[redacted]

[redacted]

Czech Fairytales

Vitalis
2005

Czech Fairytales

A selection of the most
beautiful folk tales
by Božena Němcová
and Karel Jaromír Erben

Vitalis
2005

Cover painting and illustrations: Karel Hruška
Translation: Renata Pešková
Printing and binding: Finidr, Český Těšín

ISBN 80-7253-190-5

www.vitalis-verlag.com

Contents

Preface

This volume is a selection of the most beautiful Czech fairytales that – handed down only verbally for a long time – delight, enthuse and fill with pleasant excitement since centuries. That these fairytales have not been lost over the years is mainly owing to Božena Němcová, the most important female prose writer in Bohemia and Karel Jaromír Erben, the nation's romantic poet who, like the Grimm Brothers in the German-speaking region, collected the treasure of fairytales and legends of their homeland.

Although the folktales narrated in this book remind of many a known plot and motive from other European legends and fables, they are conspicuous of an entirely unique exotic appeal. They offer an interesting insight into old Slavic myths, customs and traditions. The overall pervading trace from *Tales of the Arabian Nights* is probably owing to the Bohemian crusaders who came in contact with exotic cultures and foreign people on their crusades to the East. Along with the treasures they brought home from the Orient, they also brought all kinds of stories as "valuable booty" to the Vltava where the matter was clothed in native robes and administered a local colour.

The Black Princess

by Božena Němcová

In one country there lived a very poor fisherman. A small shanty, a little boat and a few nets – that was all his property. In spite of his poverty he lived with his wife peacefully and harmoniously. He only wished God would let him have one child at least. However, this had not yet come true.

The fisherman had the duty to supply the royal kitchen with fish. Once the King ordered him to catch many fish – and the biggest ones only – as soon as possible because he would have many guests in the castle. If the fisherman brought them, a good wage would await him. If not, he would be strictly punished. The fisherman knew the King. He knew that the King always kept his word. So he did not delay, he took the nets, jumped into the little boat and set to the sea. He had floated several hours already but he had not taken out the full net. He only caught a few tiny fish. He threw them back sullenly because he did not want them even for his own dinner. He was beginning to get frightened. Evening was coming and he did not have a single big fish. And still there were shoals swarming around him as if they were teasing him. As soon as he spread the net, they were away and came up at the other side of the boat.

"There must be a spell on you," he said almost crying after he pulled up the empty net again. "I have been fishing for a good many years but this has not happened to me yet. What shall I do! I hoped to earn something but as I see it now, I will be punished."

"Easy help, my friend," somebody said behind him. The scared fisherman turned and saw a man, all black, behind him as if he had fallen from heaven. His breath was taken away and he had an icy feeling when he had a look at the man.

"Why are you afraid?" the unknown man said when he saw the fisherman's fear. "I will not do anything to you. I came to help you if you fulfil my wish, too."

The fisherman thought that an evil ghost was sitting with him in the boat. But when he saw that the ghost was in a good mood, he promised to do everything he could do, only if he helped him with the fish.

"All right," answered the black man. "If you give me what you do not know of at home, you will have your boat full of the

most delicious and the biggest fish immediately."

"That I give you gladly," the fisher said without thinking long. He had so few tools that he knew of everything easily.

"I will pick it up in twice seven years, then."

After that the black man took the net and as soon as he dropped it, he brought it up full of the best fish.

The fisherman was happy to escape the trouble so easily. He looked for good earnings and hurried home.

His wife was already expecting him. When she saw the little boat in the distance, she started to prepare a tasty dinner for her husband to refresh him after work. "It was a blessed catch," she said when the fisherman pushed the little boat ashore. She helped him take out the fish. "I was worried whether you would succeed. The King sent servants twice already to ask when you would come."

"I was worried, too, dear wife. But I think that the King will be satisfied." He prepared everything, ate dinner and went to sleep because he wanted to bring the fish to the castle early in the morning.

The King was afraid that the best food would be missing at the feast. So he was pleased when the fisherman rushed in with such nice fish, and rewarded him properly.

The fisherman wanted to please his wife after some time again and bought her a beautiful skirt. The wife was not a little astonished. She examined the skirt and said:

"I must also please you as you have remembered me so nicely." After that she confided to the man that their many-year-long wish has been fulfilled. Yet the fisherman did not rejoice so much as his wife had expected. He remembered the former day. First now he recognized what the black man had wheedled out of him. Not to sadden the poor mother, he did not want to mention it at all. He overcame himself and hid the sorrow in his heart.

The time went quickly away and the fisherman's wife gave birth to a son. The parents liked to see him and so they gave him the name Radovid. The little boy was so lovable that the fisherman cheered up, too. He forgot his sorrow a little.

Before long the boy went to the sea with his father and picked up shells that lay on the shore. When he was bigger, he helped weave nets. He was also lucky several times and caught fish for his mother for dinner. Twice seven years ran away and the fisherman almost did not

notice. In the joy over his jaunty son he forgot the black guest. But the black man was not so forgetful.

The fisherman's wife called her son to breakfast once in the morning but in vain. She thought that he had set to hunt so she asked the father. But he did not know anything either. Immediately the father remembered the black man. He lamented and accused himself of not paying better attention. With great pain he told his wife the sad story. The poor parents moaned but they did not catch the black man's ear. He put a sack of gold in the shanty instead of him. They did not scorn it, even though they knew that it was a bad compensation for the beloved child.

Far far away from the fisherman's shanty there was a golden castle under the ground where an enchanted princess lived. She was exceedingly wonderful but as black as coal. Reputedly, a powerful magician saw her once who had fallen in love with her. She rejected him though. He put a spell on her and she became black. She would stay black until a lad fell in love with her who would leave his home and undergo various dangers for his love of her. That would not be such a tough spell, had he not left her in the underground land. What could she do there? Who could rescue her from there?

One day the princess walked in the garden and cried. Suddenly a dwarf appeared in front of her and asked her why she was crying. The princess stopped and stared at the weird figure. Yet he asked her kindly so she told him everything about her.

"Do not worry about that," he said after he listened to her. "If only a lad is the problem, I will find him myself. But what if he does not like you and would not like to stay here?"

"Then there is no help for me and I will stop worrying."

"And will you marry me?"

"You?" the princess said and looked down derisively at the manikin.

"Why are you looking at me like this?"

The princess was afraid to make him angry and thus thwart the only hope for her release. She answered him kindly: "If you bring the lad here and do not behave intrusively, I promise you this: If the lad does not want to love me and he does not want to stay here, I will marry you." She calmed the dwarf this way. He promised everything and left.

Then he changed into a black man, departed for the world and wheedled the ill-considered promise out of the fisherman. So we

know how long the princess had to wait. But she did not think it to be so long. The years run quicker under the ground and she stayed young.

One day the dwarf appeared again and fulfilled his promise: he brought a lad to the princess. He did not take him into his power against his will. He tempted him for so long until the lad left with him voluntarily. It was Radovid.

He liked the underground land. Everything was the same as on the Earth, only the sea was missing. Even the sun rose, only in reverse. When it was night on the Earth, under the ground it was day. The castle was made of pure gold and was beautifully decorated. When the sun shone behind it nobody could look at it due to the glisten. There was a garden round the castle in which unseen flowers swayed silently,

birds with many-coloured feathers flew among trees of which branches bowed to the ground heavy with delicate fruits. Wherever he looked he saw beauty everywhere. He did not have to do anything. When he wished for something it was fulfilled immediately. No wonder he did not long for his home! Of course he often thought of his mother and father. But the princess was with him all the time and when she noticed his homesickness she did her best to please him. She sang him sweet songs, led him round the garden and told him various stories. Even his mother could not care for him more or love him more. Yet Radovid loved the princess, too, no matter that she was black. The years ran by in all this pleasure and he did not know where they had gone. One thing he was sure of: he loved the princess more and more and he could not live without her. And so the days passed happily.

One morning the princess noticed dark clouds on her darling's face. She asked him what was the matter.

Radovid told her: "You know how I love you and so you will forgive me for my plea. My parents loved me completely as I was their only son. I have never thought about how great a loss it would have been for them when I disappeared. It worries me now how little I cared about them. Let me see them. I will return to you forever after that."

The princess was not glad to hear it but she could not refuse his plea as she wanted to fulfil all the conditions of her release.

"I agree," she said. "But you must promise something to me and both your and my happiness or misfortune will depend on it."

Radovid consented.

Then the princess said: "You mustn't mention a word to anybody where you have been the whole time. You mustn't say to anybody that you have a wife. You mustn't promise your love to anyone else. If you do not keep this, you will be unhappy. You will probably not see me any more and I will lose all hope for my release."

She blew a silver trumpet three times and the dwarf appeared in front of them. "Guide Radovid to where you brought him from," the princess ordered. Then she kissed Radovid once more, gave him the silver trumpet and said: "Remember my words: when you miss me, blow this trumpet and the dwarf will bring you to me."

After that she went to her chamber. Radovid was so deep in thought on the way that he did not notice which way the

dwarf was leading him. Before he awoke from his thoughts, they were at the sea, at the place where his home used to be. There his guide left him.

Radovid entered the shanty. When he did not find his parents there he asked about them. "Dear lad, the fisherman has been away for many years. He lives in a beautiful house in the town and he has much money. But nobody knows where he got it," they told him in the shanty. So Radovid made for the town. There people showed him a magnificent house that belonged to the former fisherman.

Without much thinking he entered his father's house and asked for lodgings. The old fisherman, a rich lord now, welcomed him warmly and invited him to the table. Radovid was hungry and the invitation came in handy.

When he entered the hall, he saw his mother with a girl whom she treated as her own daughter. They all sat together at the table, ate and talked. But as it was not the custom to ask a guest about his name, state and work, they did not know yet who the stranger was.

"Is this your daughter?" Radovid asked his mother and pointed to the girl.

"Yes, but not our own. We had only one son yet we lost him when he was fourteen."

"How did it happen?"

"You do not want to know, sir. It is too sad."

"Would you recognize him if he came to you?"

"Well, we would not. He must be quite tall, approximately as you are."

"You guessed, dear mother. I am your son."

The parents exclaimed, embraced him and kissed his handsome face. The ward spread the news in the house meanwhile so that everybody who was within reach rushed in and they wanted to see the son of their good lord. The joy continued long. When everything got quieter, the parents asked the son where he was and what had happened to him. But Radovid remembered his lover's words far too well. He did not reveal anything. He only asked them to be satisfied that he had come back.

The mother was calmer when she thought her son to be lost. As soon as it turned out that the handsome lad was her son, thousands of thoughts swarmed in her mind of how to marry him. She decided eventually that she would give him their ward for a wife. She did not consider if he would want her, too. She was sure that he would like her. She was a lass like apple-tree bloom. Everybody, who had seen her, liked her. Radovid admitted her prettiness but he did not forget his black beauty.

One day the old fisherman wanted to celebrate the return of his son. He invited many guests for a noisy feast.

He was a rich neighbour and a nice host, he had a handsome son and an even prettier ward – no wonder that everybody accepted the invitation. The house was full of guests. They ate, drank and danced all day. Radovid was merry and he treated the women gallantly. Most of all he talked with the pretty ward. In the evening he went with her to the garden and as he was warmed up by the fiery wine, he promised more than he should. As soon as he let the ill-considered words slip out of his mouth, his senses left him and he fell on the ground. He felt as if the black princess stood before him. Her face, usually smiling, showed deep sorrow and the black eyes were overflowing with tears. "What have you done, Radovid?" she said painfully. "Now you cannot meet me any more unless you dare to set out on a journey alone and find me in my golden castle again. You would have to put on these iron shoes. If you like me so much that you undertake this, you will free me and we will be happier than ever. Otherwise you stay a beggar forever."

Radovid woke up. He would have thought it was all a dream had he not seen the iron shoes next to him and had he not been wearing shabby clothes. He lay far behind the town. It was a terrible change within a few hours!

Revered and respected as a prince he had been enjoying his parents and a pretty girl's presence. Now he had to undertake such a strict punishment due to those few words! Since the time he saw his lover in his dream he remembered all the

happy moments that he had spent with her. He was determined to find her even if she was on the edge of the world. He looked round and sought the silver trumpet but in vain for it had disappeared. So he got up, put on the iron shoes and set forth.

His poor parents did not know meanwhile what had happened to their son that he had disappeared so unexpectedly. The ward did not hide what he had said to her and how suddenly he disappeared from her.

Everybody thought that he would come back. But he returned neither the first nor the second nor the third day.

Eventually they started to think that a ghost in their son's shape had cheated them and that it had not been Radovid. That calmed them and they lived as before.

The troubled Radovid walked meanwhile in the iron shoes from town to village, over hill and dale until he came to a black sea. He had himself ferried and he asked the ferryman on the way if he had not heard of the golden castle.

"I never have," the ferryman answered. "But there is an island not far from here where a giant lives and he knows a lot. He may be able to tell you." The ferry landed at the island and Radovid started to look for the giant.

He really found him. He asked him then if he knew the golden castle.

"Nay, I don't know, little man, I can't help you. But if you go seven times seven days and nights, you come to a mountain where my brother lives. Hopefully, he will tell you."

"Oh poor me, what else do I have to suffer before I get there. Yet it serves me good, I should obey."

With such moaning Radovid strode on. The way led him through pleasant landscapes, across wonderful islands. Yet the grassy carpet did not attract him anywhere to have a rest and the scent of various flowers did not beguile him. The desire for the black princess drove him further and further and it did not let him rest. After he had been going seven times seven days and nights, he came to the mountain where the giant, the powerful king of the land, resided. Radovid found him and asked him if he knew the golden castle.

"I don't know," the giant answered. "My brother who is the king of birdlife and sends his messengers far and wide will help you best. Maybe some of the birds will give you news about the castle. After you go another seven times seven days and nights you come to the green sea behind which is a great black forest. It is my brother's kingdom."

Radovid thanked the giant and set on the way. After seven times seven days and nights he finally came to a green sea and he had himself ferried across it. Then he hurried to the black forest and looked for the giant, the king of birdlife. When he found him, he gave him his brother's regards and begged him to speak about the golden castle. The king gathered all his subjects immediately and asked them if one of them knew of such a castle. The little birds contemplated for a while, then a little swallow flew from the gathering, approached the king and twittered: "Oh king, I know about it."

"Which way did you fly there?"

"I bathed in seven kinds of rivers, I flew in seven kinds of forests, I saw seven kinds of mountains and then I arrived at the golden castle where the black princess dwelled."

When Radovid heard that, he thanked the king and set on the journey again. So many inconveniences did he suffer before he swam across the seven rivers, crossed the seven forests and climbed the seven mountains that it is not possible to write it all. Yet

nothing was too hard for him. He made his way in his iron shoes.

One day, after he had finally endured it all, he saw a golden castle in the distance. How he thanked God that he had reached the end of his bitter journey! Tired and weary with hunger and thirst he came to the garden, there he sat under a tree and fell asleep. Exactly at that time the black princess walked in the garden. She came to the tree where Radovid slept. In wonder she stopped and saw what man was lying there. How she cheered up when she recognized him! She saw the sun-burnt face, the shabby clothes and the skinny body that had suffered a lot. She could not wait and woke him.

When Radovid awoke and saw his lover next to him, he started to ask for pardon and promised faithful love till death. She forgave him gladly. They kissed each other warmly to settle it. As soon as lips touched lips, the princess' face began to blanch. In a short while the most charming white lady with black eyes stood before Radovid. But he would have loved her even if she stayed black.

Suddenly the dwarf appeared before them and said: "I am the magician who put the spell on you, princess. I would have loved to have you as a wife but Radovid fulfilled all conditions and

I have no right to you any more. Now you can decide if you want to stay here or go back to the Earth."

But the princess had started to like the underground place since Radovid returned so she decided to stay. Also Radovid had gone off the world so they lived happily and harmoniously separated from the world. They lived in the golden castle and they did not miss the world's pleasures until death.

The Three Spinners

by Karel Jaromír Erben

Once there was a poor widow who had an only daughter. Her name was Liduška. And since they did not have any fields, not even a single cow, they made their living on spinning. Liduška was a very pretty and well-mannered girl. However, she had one fault, she was incredibly lazy. Whenever she was supposed to sit at a spinning wheel she started crying, and if her mother finally did bring her to it then her work was not worth mentioning.

Yet once her mother grew tired of it, she became angry and smacked her. At this moment Liduška started crying and moaning so that one could hear it miles away.

At that same moment the Queen was riding past. When she heard the terrible crying, she ordered her coachman to stop, got off the coach and she entered the cottage because she thought that some disaster had happened there.

When she saw Liduška crying so sadly, she asked her: "What happened to you, my dear child?"

"Ooh, ooh, my mum has beaten me."

The Queen turned to the mother and said: "Why do you hit the poor girl?"

The mother was embarrassed and did not know how to answer. She was ashamed in front of the Queen that her daughter was so lazy.

"Oh, merciful Queen, it is very difficult with the girl because she does not want anything in her hand but the distaff and she would only sit by the spinning-wheel night and day. But today I became angry and smacked her. That is why she was crying."

The Queen became fond of this girl because she was a great lover of spinning. So she told the mother: "I tell you, Mother – as your daughter likes to spin so much, let her go with me, I will take care of her. I have a lot of beautiful linen back in the palace

and if she works as hard as at home, I promise that she will not regret it."

The mother was very happy about this and the Queen took her daughter to her palace immediately.

When they arrived at the palace, the Queen took Liduška's hand and led her to three rooms. They were full of linen, from floor to ceiling and it was so beautiful that it was shining like silver and gold and was as soft as unspun silk.

Then the Queen told the girl: "Work hard, my dear daughter, and once you have spun all this linen I will give you my son for a husband and you will become the queen."

After that the Queen had brought an expensive lovely spinning wheel which was made of ivory and the feathers on it were golden, and also an immense basket of spools of yellow perfumed cane. She left Liduška alone with the linen in one of those rooms.

When the Queen left, Liduška sat next to the window and began crying mournfully. If she spun hard for hundred years from morning to evening and from evening to morning, it would not be possible to spin all the linen that was there. And what about her who hated spinning anyway?

So she was sitting and crying the whole night and the next day till noon and she moved neither her hand nor foot.

When noon came, the Queen arrived to have a look at whether Liduška had spun a lot and she was very surprised to see that the linen had not been moved. Liduška excused herself saying that she was missing her mother and that she could not have taken anything in her hand for this grief.

The Queen believed this, she comforted her and said: “Do not be sad, my daughter, and be twice as hard-working tomorrow so that you can get my son and become the queen.”

After she left, Liduška sat by the window again, looking outside sighing and doing nothing again until the evening and till next day's noon.

The Queen came at noon and was even more surprised and frowned when she saw that Liduška had not touched the distaff by then. Liduška again made an excuse that she had got a headache after yesterday's crying and that was why she could not do anything.

The Queen was satisfied but as she was leaving, she said: “It is time, Liduška, to start working if you want to get my son and become the queen!”

That day till the evening as well as the next day in the morning it

was the same as the first and the second time: Liduška did not even notice the spinning wheel but was sitting by the window and looking outside.

The Queen opened the door again at noon and when she saw that Liduška had wasted her time, she got very angry and said: "Listen to me, Liduška, it is the last time today. If nothing is spun tomorrow once again, I will not give you my son, I will also have you locked in a black tower. There are many frogs, snakes and scorpions. I will let you starve to death so that you do not deceive me and waste my time any longer."

Then the Queen turned around angrily, slammed the door and left.

Then Liduška began to feel uneasy! Cold sweat ran down her forehead only from the thought of tomorrow. What should she do? She prepared her distaff, sat at the spinning wheel and started spinning. But how could she spin when she was so incredibly lazy! So she put her work away and sat by the window. She was crying so much that her heart almost broke by the evening.

Suddenly somebody tapped on the window. When Liduška turned around, she saw three ugly old women standing outside. The first one's lower lip was so big that it was hanging over her chin. The second one had such a wide right-hand thumb that it was covering her whole palm. And the third one had her right foot so flat as if somebody had beaten it with a flail. When Liduška saw them, she got such a fright that she jumped away from the window. Yet these three women were smiling at her kindly and they were

showing her to open the window and not to be afraid of them.

"Good evening, beautiful girl," they said. "Why are you crying so sadly?"

Liduška took all her courage and answered in a crying voice: "How should I not cry and feel sorry for myself? I have to spin all the linen which you see here and two other rooms full from floor to ceiling." She recounted to the old women everything that had happened to her; that the Queen had promised her that once she has spun all then linen she would give her son to her and she would be the queen. "But what good is that for me?" she added. "I cannot spin it all before I die."

The old women smiled and said: "You know what, girl? If you promise us that you will invite us to your wedding and that we will sit next to you and that you will not be ashamed of us in front of the guests, then we will spin all the linen before long."

"I will be glad to do anything you wish," Liduška said merrily. "Start working soon."

So they climbed into the room through the window, they sent Liduška to bed and started spinning the linen. The one with the wide thumb was pulling the thread, the one with the long lip was licking it and straightening it and the one with the flat foot was stepping

on the peddle and was turning it round. It went as well as if it was raining.

Liduška got up in the morning when the sun rose. She saw a huge pile of lovely, straight and thin yarn on little spools and it did her heart good. And there was such a hole in the linen that she could have hidden herself in it. The old women said goodbye to Liduška and promised that they would come again in the evening. Then they left quietly through the window.

The Queen came at midday to see if Liduška had been wasting time. She was very surprised to see the pile of such beautiful yarn. Her forehead brightened and she praised Liduška for her hard work. When it started to get dark, the old women were already standing by the window and the girl opened it for them happily.

And it was like that every night – they came in the evening and left in the morning. More and more linen had gone from the room while Liduška was sleeping. In the end the first room was completely empty. And every noon when the Queen came to have a look how much Liduška had spun, she could not help admiring the lovely yarn and praise Liduška for her diligence. She often used to say: "My dear child, how much have I wronged you."

The old women had already started to work in the second room. And when this one was almost empty, the Queen started preparing the wedding. And when almost nothing was left in the third room, Liduška thanked the old women heartily for their big help.

The old women told her: "But do not forget, girl, what you have promised us. One day you will not regret it."

When all the linen from the three rooms was spun and everything was ready for the wedding the young King came. He was very pleased to have such a young, pretty and hard-working bride and said to her: "Ask me for anything you want and you will receive it all."

Liduška remembered the three old women and asked: "I have three old aunts at home. They are very poor and simple but they have done me much good. Allow me to invite them to the wedding."

The young King and the Queen gave their permission.

When the wedding day came and the guests were seating themselves, the door opened. The three old women dressed in an old-fashion, even in a funny way entered the room.

When the bride noticed them, she ran towards them and welcomed them joyfully. "Welcome, my dear aunts, welcome. Come and sit at the table next to me."

The guests were looking at each other and they would have started laughing if they were not afraid of the King. The King and the Queen went red as peony but they could not say anything to Liduška because they had given her their permission.

Liduška was putting the food on the women's plates herself and pouring drinks for them during the dinner. She was always offering things to them: "Eat and drink, my dear aunts, you have done me much good."

After dinner the guests were leaving the table. Then the young King came to the first old woman with the flat foot and asked her: "Grandma, why do you have such a flat foot?"

"From spinning, lad, from spinning."

Then he walked to the second one with the wide thumb: "But tell me Grandma, what do you have such a wide thumb from?"

"From spinning, lad, from spinning."

So he turned to the third old lady who had the long lip hanging over her chin and said: "Grandma, why do you have such a long lip?"

"From spinning, lad, from spinning."

When the young King heard all this he got frightened. He immediately ordered his beautiful wife not to touch any thread any more until she died. He did not want her to have such a flat foot and such a wide thumb and such an ugly lip hanging over the chin.

In the meantime the three old women disappeared from the room and nobody knew where to. But Liduška blessed them whenever she remembered them. And no other wife has ever kept the order of her husband so gladly and faithfully as she kept the ban of her King.

The Golden Hill

by Božena Němcová

Libor was the only son of a poor widow. After he had trained to be a gardener, he returned home. Yet as he could not find work, he went to the royal gardener, asked him for work and obtained it immediately. He was an orderly, very decent fellow and a diligent worker and everybody liked him. He worked as a journeyman in the royal garden for three years, and because he could handle his pennies, he soon saved a few gold coins. One day at noon he put down his tools and went to rest by a little pond under a willow bush. It was his favourite place. He lay on the soft grass, thinking what he would buy with the saved money. He looked up to the sad mourning willows, and saw their bent tops watching themselves on the bluish surface of the pond as a virgin in the eye of her lover. There was a sudden noise, and light splashing of water was to be heard in a moment. Libor pushed the thick wicker apart and looked to see what happened. He saw three maidens bathing in the pond. Two of them were beautiful, but the third one was magnificent. As soon as Libor saw her, his head began to spin and his heart began to beat so much that it almost flew from his body.

The maidens did not have the slightest idea that somebody was watching them. They swam for a short while, then they went out to the river bank, dressed in white suits and having gathered their veils, they changed into swans and flew away. When the maidens were dressing, Libor's soul

dwelled in his eyes. Immediately after they changed into swans, he jumped up and stretched his arms after them as if he wanted to stop the fleeing creatures.

When there was no sign of the swans, Libor went to the place where the luscious maiden had sat. He knelt on the grass and put his face to the place where he saw her tiny footprints. He would have lain long this way if the gardener had not come for him. In his whole life he had not worked in such a scatterbrained way as he did that half-day. He did not see nor hear anybody and did not say a word to anybody.

Libor pondered about everything in the night and decided to be smarter if the maidens came the next day. He waited for the next day with inexpressible desire. As soon as noon came, he went to the pond and hid close to the place where the maidens' clothes lay the day before. It did not take long, three swans came and having changed into maidens, they started to strip. They put their white clothes close to Libor. Yet the most charming hung her veil just above his head. As soon as Libor heard them splashing in the water, he held out his hand and slipped the veil off the twig. The leaves rustled, the maidens took fright, jumped out onto the river bank, put their clothes and veils on and soon the swan wings rustled in the air. Yet the most charming one was not among them, she ran on the river bank and looked for her veil for she could not change into a swan without it.

"Have birds carried it away, wind blown it away or a bad man taken it from me?" So the poor maiden moaned and wept. Suddenly Libor came out of the bushes.

"Tell me, lad," the maiden asked him and stepped towards him, "have you not seen my white veil? It got lost and I do not know where it is."

"Birds have not carried it away nor wind blown away. I hid it on my breast."

"Oh, I beg you then to give it back to me. I must follow my sisters."

"Not at all, charming lady. You will not receive your veil and don't you dare go away. I love you more than the whole world, more than my mother, more than myself. If you do not stay, I will die of grief." When saying those words, Libor took the maiden's hand and looked into her eyes so longingly that she listened gladly.

"Do not ask me, lad, to stay with you. It would bring you bad luck. My mother would come for me and it would be all over for you."

"Let her come! I would fight with giants, jump into fire or withstand any evil for you. Please, stay with me."

"I will stay, then. What is your name?"

"Libor. And yours?"

"Čekanka."

"Come, my dear Čekanka, I will lead you to my mother. She will love you as if you were her own daughter. I am not rich though, but I will work day and night for you. I will provide anything that you may wish."

Arm in arm they went to Libor's mother. The old woman wondered when she saw her son coming with such a beauty. And she wondered more hearing that she was his bride. She welcomed her kindly and weeping blessed the young couple.

"Now, my rose," Libor said after they had enjoyed some time together, "I must go to work again. What should I bring to you in the evening to please you?"

"It is enough when you come yourself. Go, my Libor, and come back soon."

Libor met his mother in the hall. Taking a veil from his breast, he gave it to her saying: "Dear Mother, hide the veil into the coffer and do not give it to Čekanka even if she asks for it. Treat her as a spring flower so that she does not shrivel."

Mother hid the veil and went to the bride. Although she did not know where she came from

and who she was, she did not ask. She believed that her son would not choose any maiden that would not be worth him. As soon as she entered the chamber, she sat next to Čekanka and told many things about her homestead, about good and bad qualities of her little Libor. "I have told him many times to marry," she finished her speech, "but I cannot believe that he has obeyed so soon. I thought that he had been leading our princess when he came with you."

"And if Libor did not take my veil from me, you would see even bigger beauty, Mother. Its charm is exceptional and it matches the dress in a pleasing way. It is a pity that Libor has taken it away. He will have to lend it to me for a while so that you can see me wearing it."

"He did not carry it away. He entrusted it to my protection and said not to give it to you."

"I do not want it. Does he, silly lad, think that I long for it? I only wanted to show you, Mother, how I look in it."

"Wait, girl, I will bring it and put it on you. Then I will hide it again and Libor will not suspect anything."

The old woman turned, went to the coffer and brought the veil. Čekanka took it off her hands eagerly and unfolding it, touched it with pleasure. Suddenly she stepped to a window, opened it and turning to Mother she said: "Tell Libor, Mother, that if he wants to marry me, he must come for me to the Golden Hill." Having said that she put the veil on her head and, changing into a swan she flew away through the window.

The poor old woman was scared stiff. She was afraid of what Libor would say when he came home.

Evening was coming and Libor hurried home. He carried a beautiful bouquet in one hand and a basket full of the most delicious fruits in the other one. His cheeks shone with bliss and his eyes burnt. As the old woman saw him passing the window, she began to tremble with fear. There came Libor into the door and examining the chamber he asked:

"Where is Čekanka?"

Mother said in tears what had happened and what Čekanka had

said. Colour faded out from the lad's shining face with every word. He had his hands on his breast that was held by immense pain, and looked at the place where he had sat with his darling. He could not think. Then after a long while he breathed deeply and tears like big beads poured down his cheeks.

"Mother, prepare a bundle for me, I will go to the Golden Hill," were his first words after a long silence.

"My dear son, do not do that to me, what shall I do without you? Forget the girl who cheated you this way."

"Do what I have said, Mother. I cannot be without Čekanka. I must find her, should I travel through the whole world."

In vain was his mother's moaning. Libor took some money, the tied bundle, said farewell to his mother and went to seek the Golden Hill.

"But where shall I find it?" he thought walking across a field. He took a direct way where his eyes led him. He wandered long until he came to a dreadful forest from which he did not know the way out. His feet hurt, he suffered from hunger and thirst and there were no signs of people. All of a sudden he heard barking of a dog. He thought that he would find a human dwelling. And he found it after a while. Very pleased he entered the cottage where an old gamekeeper lived.

"Please," Libor started to speak, "let me have a short rest and give me a piece of bread. I got lost in the forest and I have not eaten or drunk for a long time."

"Sit down on the bench. I give you what I have," the old man answered. He brought a loaf of bread and a piece of game and gave it to Libor. A serving from the royal table would not have been more delicious to Libor than that dark bread and meat.

"Where do you go, son?" the gamekeeper asked after a while.

"To the Golden Hill," Libor answered and immediately started to tell everything to the gamekeeper. He asked the old man if he knew where such a hill stood.

"Dear son, I do not know but I can ask." He opened the door, took a whistle and blew three times. There came a hundred crows and they all flapped their wings around his head.

"Tell me, you wanderers, if any of you know of the Golden Hill."

"We do not know but our friends that are with your brother, they will surely know."

"Go, son, to my brother. He lives a hundred miles from here in a forest. Tell him that I greet him and that he should tell you where the Golden Hill is."

Libor thanked the gamekeeper for his hospitality and the piece of good advice and after parting with him he wandered on. It takes a pretty long time to stride one hundred miles. Yet everything has its end. Libor reached the goal of his way, too. It was a forest again where the gamekeeper's brother lived. He welcomed Libor with friendliness and having heard greetings from his brother, he took out a whistle immediately and whistled. There came two hundred crows that floated flapping round him.

"Which of you will tell me where the Golden Hill is?" the gamekeeper asked them.

"None of us knows of the Golden Hill but our sisters at your brother's will surely know of it."

"Have you heard, son, what they said?" the gamekeeper told Libor. "There is no other way. You must go another two hundred miles to my brother and ask him about the Golden Hill. Yet have a rest first and refresh yourself."

After that the gamekeeper turned and brought bread, meat and wine to the guest. Libor enjoyed the

meal, thanked the old man warm-heartedly and went on. When a person hurries up merrily, the way passes swiftly. That happened to our wanderer, too. He left the two hundred miles behind him quicker than he had expected. He had the cottage, where the third brother lived, in front of him soon. "If he sends me away without a piece of news, I do not know where to turn," Libor thought to himself entering the cottage. The third brother welcomed him as kindly as the other two brothers and having understood what was claimed he called his three hundred crows with his whistle.

"I would like to know where the Golden Hill is. Who of you knows of it, tell me quickly," the gamekeeper asked his messengers.

A single one stepped forward and she was limping. This one told her lord:

"I know of the Golden Hill. It stands in the centre of a nice valley three hundred miles from here and it glitters from afar. There is a golden castle built on it. In the castle lives a witch with her three daughters. She is an evil woman. Once I wanted to have a closer look at that castle but as soon as the crone saw me she took a stone, threw it ten yards and broke my leg. Since that time I limp."

"Serves you right. Why do you enter where your inquisitiveness pushes you. Yet I will send you there myself. You will carry my guest to the foot of the hill on your wings. Stay here. The rest of you shall leave." The black-feathered wanderer did not like it somehow but she could not say a word. The lord punished disobedience very strictly. After Libor ate what the game-keeper offered him, they shook hands, Libor wished the game-keeper all the best and parted. He went first and the crow after him. About twenty steps behind the cottage the crow shouted to him to wait. She wanted to tell him something.

"Tear three acorns," she said, "and hide them properly. When we fly and I cry: 'Drop an acorn,' do so."

Libor obeyed her advice, tore the acorns and hid them. After that she ordered him to mount her. When he did so, she soared with him high above the dark pinewood. As clouds move, forests, fields, villages and townes passed by in front of his eyes. Suddenly they were at the end of the country. In front of them there was a vast blue-green sea surface glittering. When they were far behind the shore, the crow cried: "Drop an acorn!" Libor took it out of the pocket and dropped it into the sea. A big wide spread oak grew off the water immediately. The crow with Libor descended to its top.

"Here we have a rest. My wings are tired and it will take long before we reach the end of the sea," the crow said having sat next to Libor. Yet she got up again after a while and they went on quickly. As they flew, the oak disappeared. Before they reached the end of the sea, Libor dropped the two other acorns into the sea. Every time oaks grew from them on which the wanderers rested.

Behind the sea there was a high mountain. The crow descended on it.

"It is another hundred miles from this mountain to the Golden Hill," she said to Libor. "The worst part is over. Therefore find for yourself how to get there. I will return home because I do not wish to lose the second leg," she said and in a minute she was in the air.

Libor watched the deceitful crow angrily. All of a sudden he heard tremendous shouting. He climbed down the hill to see what was happening. And he wondered very much when he saw two tyrannical giants fighting. Yet they noticed him immediately. They stopped fighting for a while and shouted to him: "How dare you, you earthly worm, to enter our kingdom?"

"I came across a vast sea and rested on this mountain. I heard tremendous shouting. As I did not know what it was nor that I should not enter, I climbed down."

"If it is so, you are pardoned. Now go away so that we can decide our quarrel."

"Can I ask you what is the matter I have heard a lot and I may serve you with a piece of good advice."

"Go your way, why should you advise us. We know everything," one of them answered back.

"Do not go," the other one ordered, "I will tell you about the quarrel and gladly listen to your advice. Look, there lies a saddle that we two brothers inherited from our father. It has a unique quality. Whoever sits on it and says: 'I want to be there and there!', will appear there immediately. No wonder we both want it now. We could not solve the problem on good terms so we decided that he who could overcome the other one would obtain the saddle."

"I will make peace for you soon, only let me have a look at the saddle," Libor said and stepped closer to the fateful object. The giants looked to see what he

would do. However, he sat on the saddle suddenly and said: "I want to be on the Golden Hill!" and there was no sign of him. The giants' trial was finished.

In a moment Libor appeared on the Golden Hill at the gate of the golden castle. He rolled down and knocked on the gate. The bar opened and an ugly crone came out asking Libor what he wanted.

"I seek my darling called Čekanka. If she is here and if you are the mistress of this castle, lead me to her."

"Not so gruffly, boy! I am the mistress of this castle and Čekanka is my daughter. Do not think that you can gain her so easily."

"And what shall I do to deserve her?"

"You must fulfil three things. If you manage, Čekanka will be yours, if you do not, you will die."

"Whatever you order, I will fulfil."

"Then come with me," the ugly crone said and led Libor across the marble court into beautiful chambers. She ordered him to wait in one of them and left. The

door opened in a short while and Čekanka stood on the threshold. With one jump came Libor to her and embraced her.

"Oh, I longed for you so much, my darling. Why did you not stay at my place, why did you cause me such great grief? Who knows now if I will obtain you from your mother?"

"If I stayed at your place, you would have to undertake even more evil. Do not worry and trust in me as I have trusted in you. The end will be happy."

So pleased Čekanka her faithful lover and left. The night was coming near to its end, Libor obtained a tasty supper and then lying in soft cushions he fell into a deep sleep. In the morning, when he was hardly dressed, the old crone came to him, brought him his breakfast and said: "If you want to obtain Čekanka, come quickly with me. I will assign you the first task."

She did not have to tell Libor twice. He went quickly after the crone to the yard. She gave him a wooden saw, axe and club and led him to a large pinewood not far from the castle.

"At this place," she said, "I want to have a hundred fathoms of wood until evening. If you are not ready, you must die."

Libor felt like crying rather than like working. What could he do with the wooden tools? He took the axe, hit a trunk and only a handle remained in his hand. The same happened with the saw. Flinging the tools on the ground he lay on the moss. He listened to the singing of birds and thought about Čekanka. He remembered several times that his death was near. Yet he believed in his lover's words because she had promised him that she would not leave him. Noon came and Čekanka brought his lunch.

"Look, I had supposed that you would be in the middle of your work and you are resting."

"How should I work when both the saw and the axe are broken? There is no other help but my death."

"Do not speak of it. Have you forgotten what I had said? Sit and eat, I will work myself."

Having finished her speech, she took a few steps, turned her ring which glittered on her long finger three times and said: "Here at this place I want to have a hundred fathoms of wood!" At that time one could hear cutting, chopping, sawing, and before Libor had finished his lunch, a hundred fathoms of wood were arranged.

Libor wondered about the great power of his lover. From then on he was not afraid of anything. They talked for a while. Čekanka forbade Libor to tell anything to her mother and went home. The crone came in the evening and froze with anger seeing that what she had ordered, was ready. She led Libor home and brought him dinner into his chamber herself. The next day in the morning Libor received two forged buckets and and he had to follow the crone again. They came to a large pond and the crone said: "You will pour over water from this pond to that hill, or I kill you."

Libor sat on the ground and waited for noon. Why should he strive and pour over the water pointlessly. Čekanka came with his lunch at noon again. "As I see, you have not worked much," she spoke.

"I waited for your help. What shall my labour do."

Čekanka turned her ring saying: "I want water from this pond to pour over to that hill and stay there till the sunset." At that moment water disappeared from the pond and the hill was soaked from top to foot. Libor thanked his lover with a warm kiss and she hurried home. The crone gnashed her teeth because her intention had not come true when she saw water on the hill in the evening. Libor dined at home happily and went to bed.

When he got up in the morning, he had to follow the crone to the green meadow again. When she came to the middle, the crone took a whistle and blew it. Three hundred hares came as if grasshoppers were jumping on the meadow.

"You will pasture the hares on this meadow till the evening. If a single one is lost, I will kill you." But as soon as she turned away, there was no trace of them.

"Only a fool would try to catch them. Čekanka will call them for me," Libor said. And exactly that happened. When Čekanka came, she turned her ring and ordered that the hares return to the meadow and stay there till the evening. In that moment the meadow was full of them and not a single one was missing.

The crone burnt with anger when she saw the hares on the meadow in the evening and Libor sitting among them as if butter would not melt in his mouth.

"So Čekanka is mine now?" Libor asked when they came to the castle.

"You can take her tomorrow," the furious crone answered.

When there was silence in the whole castle, there was a sound on Libor's window: "Coo, coo, coo!" Libor jumped out of the bed,

went to the window and saw a cute little dove. “Lo, what are you looking for here?”

“What should I be looking for but you. I am your Čekanka,” the little dove answered sitting on his shoulder and pecking him on his cheeks. “I bring you a piece of good advice which you ought to follow tomorrow. Mother will lead you to a hall where will stand three hundred maidens with identical faces and clothes. You will be set to choose me from them. If you want to recognize me, pay good attention to eyes. She who winks with her right eye, take her, it will be me.”

“Thank you, dear little dove, even though I would recognize you among thousand maidens.”

“Do not believe that. You will see tomorrow.”

The little dove flew away and Libor anticipated the dawn peacelessly. As soon as he finished his breakfast, the crone came for him and led him to a large hall. It was so glittering and beautiful that his eyes were popping. The moon and thousands of stars made of diamonds shone on the ceiling. Long mirrors hung around on the walls and below them stood sofas covered with red velvet and silver flowers. The floor was

made of golden and silver tables. Yet what was the lustre of all those stars on the golden ceiling compared to the lustre of eyes of the lovable faces of the three hundred maidens shining to Libor. The silverwoven robes rustled across the hall. As if white swans passed by Libor, the maidens passed him and each looked into his eyes for a while. Libor thanked Čekanka in his mind for the piece of good advice, for he would indeed not know which one to choose if the last one did not wink impishly with her right eye.

"This one is mine," he said, taking Čekanka's rounded shoulder.

"Keep her, then. However, you cannot leave the castle before tomorrow dawn," the witch said.

Libor was willing to do anything now when he had what he had claimed. When he came to his chamber with his lover, he asked her if she had so many sisters.

Yet she answered: "I do not have so many sisters, only two of them. The rest of the maidens were dryads conjured up by my mother. They would tear you into pieces in a while if you had chosen one of them."

"So many times you saved my life, oh beautiful maiden!" Libor cried and kissed the albescent forehead. "Yet your mother must be a living dragon."

"Of course she is. I am still afraid that she will do something bad to you and therefore I will stay with you all the time."

Half of the day she did not move from him. Eventually, in the evening she went to her chamber saying first: "If I hear anything fishy, I will come for you and we both run away."

Love and terror would not let Libor fall asleep. At midnight there was a light rap on the window. Libor woke up immediately and opened the window. The white swan descended to the chamber and changing into Čekanka she said: "Quickly, Libor, hold my waist, put your head to mine, we will cover ourselves with the veil to be able to fly away. Mother wants to kill you tomorrow."

Libor obeyed immediately and held Čekanka's slim body. She put the veil on both heads and the two swans flew through the window down the Golden Hill where two pairs of shoes and a casket lay. The swans changed there again and Čekanka told her darling: "You will put on one pair of the shoes and I will put on the other one. They are twelve-mile boots that I took away from Mother. I have jewels in this casket, pay attention to them."

Boots on their feet and holding hands they started to pace. As they made one step, they were twelve miles further, so the way passed very quickly. However, the crone heard some rustling, got up, went to Čekanka's chamber and found nobody there. She was frightened and ran to Libor's place. It was also as empty as a bottle. Red with anger she ran for the twelve-mile shoes but they were also gone. Furiously she grabbed the twenty-four-mile shoes and made after the runaways.

"Look back, Libor, to see if there is somebody running after us," Čekanka said at the dawn.

"I see something black in the distance."

"It is my mother. Put the casket on the ground, step on it and snuggle to me." Čekanka turned her ring after these words and said: "Let my darling be a bush and me a rose on it."

In a little while the evil crone came this way as a wild lion this way but she did not notice the bush with a single blooming bud.

As soon as she disappeared, the lovers changed into their bodies and ran further. Yet the crone recognized that she had gone the wrong way. She turned and traced them again.

"Look back, Libor, who is after us?" Čekanka asked in a dark forest.

"I do not see anything but I can hear a rustle in the distance."

"It is my mother. Step on the casket!" She turned her ring three times again and said: "Let my darling be a little church and me a pulpit in it!"

The crone came in a fury again but she noticed neither the little church nor the pulpit. The lovers were glad and hurried on. But the dragon sniffed again that she had not gone the right way and returned.

"Look back, Libor, who is after us?" Čekanka asked on a large meadow.

"I see something black."

"It is my mother, step on the casket." She turned her ring three times again and said: "Let my darling be a pond and me a swan on it."

That happened immediately but the crone saw it from the distance. When she came to the pond, she changed into an ox and started to drink water from the pond. The poor swan floated almost on a land and thought that the old witch would swallow her any minute. Yet all of a sudden the swollen ox burst and water streamed back to the pond.

The little swan waved her wings merrily and they both became Libor and Čekanka again.

They did not want to look at the ugly dead body of the unnatural mother so they went a bit further. Now they did not have to be afraid of anything and had a rest for an hour. Then they hurried home cheerfully.

Libor's mother was weak and worn from worry. She had thought about her son day and night, about where he could be and if she would see him before she died. One day, as had happened a long time ago when Libor first brought his bride, the beautiful maiden turned up at the window, the door opened and Libor and Čekanka entered. The old mother would have fainted if the son had not caught her.

"Come, Mother, give the shanty to somebody, we have another residence for you," Libor said when she had freshened up a little and was talking with them.

On realising that her son had a princedom, she gave the shanty to a poor woman and went with her darling. Behind the shanty stood a carriage with four horses. They got in and at a gallop they flew to the castle that Libor and Čekanka bought on the way home. Libor lived happily with his wife and their love lasted until death. The granny was rejuvanated by her son's happiness and swang her grandchildren on her knees.

The Devil and Kate

by Božena Němcová

In one village there once lived an old maid whose name was Kate. She had a small house, a garden and besides it a few golden coins. But even if she sat all in gold, the poorest fellow would not marry her. She was bad and pert as a devil. She had an old mother and sometimes she needed to help with her. But if someone needed a penny to save his live and Kate would pay him with ducats, he would not do the least for her. She argued and quarreled about every word so loudly that it was possible to hear it from miles away. In addition to all that she was not pretty and so she was left on the shelf until she was almost forty years old.

Usually there is a ball in a village every Sunday afternoon and so it was here. As soon as the bagpipe sounded at the village magistrate's or in the pub, the chamber quickly filled with lads. Maidens stood at the backyard and the children were at the windows. The very first among them all was Kate. The lads nodded to maidens and these went to dance. Kitty had never had luck in her life although she would pay for the piper herself. Despite this she did not miss a single Sunday. One day she went to the ball and thought on her way: "I am so old and I have not yet danced with a lad. Isn't it a shame? Sincerely, I would dance even with a devil today!"

Full of anger she came to the pub, sat at the stove and watched who took whom to dance. Suddenly a man in a gamekeeper's dress entered, sat at a table close to Kitty and ordered a beer. A servant-girl brought the beer; the man took it and carried it to Kitty to drink to her. Kitty wondered silently for a while why the man did her such honor. She simpered a while but then she drank gladly. The man put the mug down, took a ducat out of his pocket, threw it to the bagpiper and called: "Solo, lads!" The lads arranged around the room and the man took Kate to dance.

"Oh gosh, who might that be?" asked the old and put their heads together. Lads grinned and maidens hid their heads behind each other and covered their mouths with their pinafores not to show Kate that they laughed at her. But Kate did not see anybody. She was merry because she danced. If the whole world laughed at her, she would not mind. The man danced only with Kate the whole afternoon and the whole evening. He bought her marzipan and sweet drinks and when the time came to go home, he walked with her in the village.

"If only I could dance with you until I die as I did today," said Kate when they should part.

"That may easily happen. Join me."

"Where do you stay?"

"Hold me tightly, I will show you."

Kate grabbed him but at the same moment the man changed into a devil and flew with her straight to hell. He stopped at the gate and knocked. The devils came, opened and when they saw how plodding their fellow was, they wanted to ease him and take Kate from him. But she stuck to him as a tick and they could not pull her away with all their might. Willy nilly the devil had to go to Satan.

"Who are you bringing?" the lord asked.

So the devil told how he had walked on the Earth and how he had heard Kate wailing about a dancer. He wanted to deter her a little so he started to dance with

her. He wanted, too, to show her round hell for a while. "I did not know," he finished, "that she would not want to let me go."

"That's because you are a fool and you don't remember my warnings," the old Satan inveighed against him.

"Before you start something with somebody you should know his thoughts. If you had remembered this when you walked Kate, you wouldn't have taken her with you. Now go away and see to it that you get rid of her."

Sullenly the devil shuffled to Earth with the maiden Kitty. He promised her miracles if she would let him go, he cursed her, but it was of little use. Weary and angry he came to a meadow with his burden where a young shepherd wrapped in an enormous fur-coat pastured sheep. The devil had changed into an ordinary man so the shepherd did not recognize him. "Whom are you carrying, friend?" he asked the devil confidentially.

"Oh dear man, I can hardly breathe. Consider this: I was going my way thoughtlessly, when the dame jumped on my back and she does not want to let me go in any way. I wanted to carry her to the nearest village and there get rid of her somehow. But I am not capable of it, my legs are sinking with fatigue under me."

"Well, wait a minute. I will help you to get rid of the insistent person but not for long because I have to pasture after that again. I will carry her half of the way"

"I would be glad."

"Do you hear? Get hold of me," the shepherd cried to Kate.

As soon as Kate heard him, she let the devil go and grabbed the bushy fur-coat. Now the slim shepherd had a burden to carry – Kate and the horrible big fur-coat that he had borrowed from the bailiff. He started to regret it soon so he pondered how he could get rid of Kate. He came to a pond and there the idea struck him to throw her into it. But how? If only he could strip both Kate and the fur-coat! The fur-coat was loose enough so he tried slowly to see if it would be possible. And look! He took out one arm and Kate did not know anything. He took out the other one and Kate still did not know anything. He removed the first tag from the button; he replaced the second one, the third one and splash! Kate lay in the pond together with the fur-coat.

The devil did not follow the shepherd. He sat on the ground, pastured the sheep and looked to see if the shepherd was coming back with Kate. He did not have to wait long. The shepherd hurried to the meadow with the wet fur-coat on his shoulder. He thought that the stranger would probably be at the village already and the sheep would be alone. When they saw each other they stared in surprise. The devil wondered why the shepherd was coming without Kate. The shepherd wondered why the man was still sitting there. When they explained the matter, the devil said to the shepherd: "Thank you. You did me a great favour. Otherwise I would have carried Kate until the Day of the Last Judgement. I will never forget it and I reward you richly one day. Just to let you know whom you have helped I tell you that I am a devil." He said that and disappeared. The shepherd stood dazed for a while and then he said to himself: "If all of them are as stupid as he is, it is good for us."

A young prince ruled the land where the shepherd lived. He was very rich and as he was a free lord over it all he enjoyed everything to the full extent. Day after day he enjoyed the different pleasures that the world can possibly offer. When the night fell, the singing of dissipating prodigal lads sounded from the prince' chambers. The land was administered by two governors who were not the least bit better than the lord himself was. What the prince did not want those two kept and the pitiful people did not know where they should get money. Those who had either a pretty daughter or money could not enjoy any peace as they could surely expect the prince to ask for them. And mercy for him who would not obey his will! Who could love the sovereign? The people cursed both the prince and the governors.

One day when the prince did not know what to think up he called the astronomer and ordered him to read the stars for him and his two governors. The astronomer followed and examined the stars to get to know how the lives of the wasters would finish.

"I am sorry, Your Princely Grace," he said when he was ready with his examination. Your life and the lives of your governors are in such a great danger that I am afraid to utter it."

"Speak, whatever it should be! However, you must stay here. If your words do not come true, you will lose your head."

"Well, listen: when the moon is in its second quarter, a devil will come for both of the governors this and this hour of that and that day. He will come for you at the full moon. He will carry you alive to hell."

"Put the lying swindler in prison!" the prince ordered and so the servants did.

Yet the prince did not feel what he pretended to. The astronomer's words shocked him like the voice of the Last Judgement. His conscience awakened in him for the first time! The governors stayed half-dead. None of them could eat a mouthful. They took all their property, sat in coaches and went home. They had their castles sealed off from all sides so that the devils could not come for them. The prince turned to the right way of living. He lived quietly and calmly and slowly started to govern the land hoping that the cruel destiny may not come true. The poor shepherd had no idea of these things. He pastured his flock day after day and did not care a bit about what was happening in the world. One day the devil stood in front of him suddenly and told him: "I came, shepherd, to reward you for your service. When the second quarter of the moon comes, I should carry the former governors of the land to hell because they

exploited the poor people and advised the prince wrongly. But as I see that they have improved I will leave them here and reward you on the same day. When that and that day comes, go to the castle of the first governor. There will be many people. When the clamour starts, the servants will open the gate and I will be leading the lord away, step to me and say: 'Leave at once or it will go ill for you!' I will obey and leave. Then ask the lord to bring you two bags of gold. If he will not want to, tell him that you will call me back. Then go to the second castle, do the same thing and claim the same reward. Husband the money well and use it for good. When the full moon comes I must take away the prince himself. But I would not advise you to want to rescue him. You would have to expose your own skin." The devil finished and left.

The shepherd remembered every word. When the second quarter of the moon came, he quitted his service and went to the castle where one of the governors stayed. He came just in time. The crowds stayed there and waited to see if the devil would carry away the lord. Suddenly the desperate crying sounded, the gate opened and the black man pulled the lord away who was livid and half-dead. Then the shepherd stepped forward from the people, took the lord's arm, pushed the devil away and shouted: "Leave at once or it will go ill for you!" The devil disappeared immediately. The happy lord kissed the shepherd's hand and asked what reward he claimed. When the shepherd said that he wanted two bags of gold, the lord ordered that they should be given to him immediately.

Satisfied the shepherd went to the second castle and did as well as at the first one. It is clear that the prince came to hear of the shepherd quite soon. Anyway, he kept asking what had happened with the lords. When he heard all this, he sent a coach with four horses for the kind shepherd. When they brought him, the prince asked him urgently to take pity on him, too, and to rescue him from the infernal claws.

"Oh my lord," the shepherd answered. "I cannot promise you that, my skin is at stake here. You are a great sinner. But if you wanted to improve entirely and govern your people just, kindly and wisely as a prince should, I would try even if I should go into the fiery hell instead of you."

The prince promised everything with a sincere mind and the shepherd left with the promise that he would come at the set day.

In dread and terror the full moon was expected everywhere. As much as the people had wished the prince this destiny, so they regretted it now. Since the time he had improved, one could not wish for a kinder prince. The days pass whether you count them with pleasure or with sorrow! Before long the day was near at hand when the prince was to say good-bye to everything that pleased him. Dressed in black, pale as death the prince sat and awaited either the shepherd or the devil. All of a sudden the door opened and the black man stood before him.

"Get ready, oh prince, the hour has come and I am here for you."

Without saying a word the prince stood up and walked behind the devil to the courtyard where an enormous crowd of people stood. But the shepherd, all plodding, made his way to the devil and cried from afar:

"Escape, escape, or it will go ill for you!"

"How dare you hinder me so? You do not know what I told you?" the devil whispered to the shepherd.

"You fool, I don't care about the prince, I care about you. Kate has come and asked about you."

As soon as the devil heard of Kate, he disappeared and left the prince in peace. The shepherd laughed at him in his mind. He was glad that he could rescue the prince through this trick. For this the prince made him his very first courtier and loved him as his own brother. And he did well because the poor shepherd was a sincere adviser and the right courtier. He did not keep a penny from the four bags of gold. He helped those with it that the governors exploited.

2

Boil Pot Boil!

by Karel Jaromír Erben

In one village once lived a poor widow who had a daughter. They stayed in an old cottage with a thatched roof and they had several hens in the loft. The old one went to the forest to pick up wood in winter and strawberries in summer and they gathered ears of grain in autumn. The young one carried eggs that their hens laid to the town for sale. So they earned their living.

Once in summer the old one became quite ill and the young one had to pick up strawberries in the forest herself. They cooked a porridge of it. She took a pot and a piece of dark bread and she left. When she had the pot full of strawberries, she came to a spring in the forest. She sat down next to the spring, took out bread from the apron and started to dine. It was exactly noon.

All of a sudden an old woman appeared from nowhere. She looked as a beggar and she held a pot in her hand.

"Oh my dear lass," said the old beggar. "How I would like to eat! I have not had a mouthful of bread since yesterday morning. Would you give me a piece of your bread?"

"Why not," said the girl, "all of it if you wish. I will be able to get home. But wouldn't it be too hard for you?"

And she gave her the whole lunch.

"God bless you, my dear lass, God bless you! And because you are so kind, my lass, I must also give you something. I give you this pot. When you put it on the table at home and say: 'Boil pot boil!' it would boil you as much porridge as you would wish. And when you will think you have porridge enough, say: 'Stop pot stop!' and it stops to boil immediately. Only do not forget what you are to say."

She handed her the little pot and disappeared so suddenly that the girl did not know where.

When she came home, she told her mother what had happened in the forest. She put the pot on the table at once and said: "Boil pot boil!" She wanted to know if the old beggar had lied or not. But the porridge started to boil at the bottom of the pot immediately. There was

more and more of it and before you could count to ten, the pot was full. "Stop pot stop!" and the pot stopped to boil.

Both of them sat at that moment and ate with pleasure. The porridge was as almond. When they finished, the young one put several eggs into a basket and carried them to the town. But she had to sit there at the market for a very long time. People gave her little money for them and she did not sell them all until evening.

The old one could not wait, she wanted to eat and she had mind to taste the porridge. So she took the pot, put it on the table and said herself: "Boil pot boil!" The porridge started to boil in the pot immediately and before the old one moved, it was full.

"I must also bring a plate and a spoon," the old one said to herself and went to the pantry.

But when she returned, she stood in shock as if dazed: The porridge poured through the full spout of the pot onto the table, from the table onto the bench and from the bench onto the floor. The old one forgot what she should say to prevent the pot from boiling. She jumped to the table and put a dish on the pot. She thought she would stop the porridge. But the dish fell on the ground and broke and the porridge poured down like a flood continuously. The chamber was so full that the old one had to escape to the hall. She lamented and wailed: “Oh the unfortunate girl, what has she brought? I thought at once that it would not be anything good!”

In a while the porridge poured from the chamber across the doorsill into the hall. The more there was, the more it increased. The old one did not know how to get out of it so she climbed up to the loft in terror. She kept wailing what a thing the unfortunate girl had brought home. Meanwhile the porridge increased more and more and before long it poured through the door and the window onto the common like clouds. Who knows how it would all have finished if the young one had not luckily returned at that moment and had not cried: “Stop pot stop!”

But there was such a heap of the porridge on the common that farmers coming home from their labour could not get through in any way and had to bite their way through to the other side.

The Clever Princess

by Božena Němcová

Two craftsmen were wandering through the world. Once they came to a nice castle. They both looked into the garden through a hole in a fence and saw a wonderful princess walking. "Bořek, do you know what I wish?" the young handsome fellow asked.

"Perhaps you want to be a lord of that castle, don't you?" Bořek answered.

"Far from it! You haven't guessed. I would wish for the princess."

"Jiřík, you are not stupid. I thought only about one thing but you think both about the princess and the castle. But don't have pointless thoughts. Come, there is a good stretch of way in front of us."

"Bořek, I would give my soul to the devil if I got that princess."

"I wouldn't do that," Bořek answered and dragged Jiřík from the fence. They walked as far as a calm pinewood near a town. They lay in a shadow to let their limbs rest a little. Bořek fell asleep as soon as he lay down. Jiřík couldn't fall asleep with all his effort, thinking all the time about the wonderful princess. All of a sudden, a lad clothed in green passed by. Seeing that Jiřík didn't sleep, he stopped by him.

"I wish you good health, youngster, where are you going?" he asked Jiřík.

"We wander through the world. But I've had enough of it, one suffers as a dog."

"I can believe you. The best way to be one's own master."

"Of course, it is. If only everyone could be."

"Well, sometimes it depends just on his will."

"What about the will. People would claim a lot if it was to be fulfilled. – For example I would like to have that princess from the close castle. I have just said that I would give my soul to a devil if I got her."

"Do you mean it?"

"Of course, I do."

"Your claim is to be fulfilled. I am a devil. If you subscribe, you will be a rich prince in a quarter of an hour and you can go to the princess. She will take to you and marry you. Here is a sheet and a pen, tear your little finger and sign with your blood."

Without thinking Jiřík took a prickle and signed the devil's sheet with his blood.

"So, you are mine now. In how many years shall I come for you?"

"Well, I think in twenty years. After I have enjoyed the love of a wonderful princess and worldly pleasures for so long, I will gladly join you."

"Very well. Here is a pouch full of ducats. Take as much as you want, it will always be full. Open your bag. There are your clothes changed into princely ones. Get dressed. A few servants are waiting for you behind the pinewood with a saddled horse. Mount him, go to the castle and call yourself as a prince."

"But I cannot speak as a prince. I will give myself away in the very first moment."

"Don't worry about it. You will know everything that you can think about. You will be trusted. Go soon, before your friend wakes up."

After that the devil disappeared. Jiřík, opening the bag, really did find rich clothes and began to dress. Then he went behind the pinewood where the decked serv-

ants were coming to meet him leading a wild horse. Jiřík swang on the horse so skillfully as if he had practiced with the best groom. Finally they headed to the princely castle.

Bořek woke up meanwhile. When he did not see Jiřík next to him, he thought he had left already. So he took his things and hurried further. So we will let Bořek go where he wants, and now we will have a look to see what happened in the castle.

The young princess was still in the garden when Jiřík arrived at the castle. He let it be announced to the king that he was this and this prince from that and that land, and asked for short-time hospitality in the castle.

The King welcomed him with great respect and let servants prepare rooms for him. The servants brought there all the prince sacs and things that the devil had supplied. A magnificent feast was prepared. Jiřík dressed himself all in gold in order to attract the princess. And so it happened. As soon as the princess saw him, she took to him. Her only wish was that the handsome prince stayed at their place forever. Jiřík also had an eye only for her and spoke in a nice manner. He was pleased that the conversation was fluent and noble. After he spent a few days in the castle, he pretended

that he wanted to leave the castle, but he was quite afraid that they would let him go.

But the princess opened her heart to her father and asked him to delay the prince. Her father did so and Jiřík stayed gladly for he noticed that he was favoured. Once he was alone with the princess. He used this chance to reveal his love and when he heard that she also loved him, he went to her father and asked him for the princess. He said he did not have any kingdom because he was the youngest son of his father but he could buy the largest one in a moment. The old King blessed them without hindrance and appointed Jiřík as his co-ruler. Soon a wedding was celebrated and Jiřík was as in heaven.

People liked him because he was good and did not harm anybody without reason. The old King died a few years later and Jiřík ruled alone.

He had already two sons and a daughter and lived happily with his wife. Sometimes he remembered the devil but he always thought: "There is long time till then, perhaps something happens."

But the time passed quickly and soon there was only one year left. When Jiřík realized the short term left, he was alarmed so much that he could not sleep day or night. He walked in the castle as pale as a ghost and looked with pain at his children and at his dear wife. What can pass unnoticed by a loving wife! She often asked Jiřík what was wrong but he always talked his way out of it and never said the real cause. He did not eat the whole day and locked himself in his room so as not to see his wife's tears and to avoid her questions. In the evening the door opened itself and a lad clothed in green entered.

"Well, Jiřík," he spoke to the pale King, "do you remember that today the twenty years have passed and that you are to join me?"

"How could I forget? But you see, I must arrange many things and I have not said good-bye to my wife yet. Give me three more days."

"I will do that, and much more. Choose one thing every day, be it anything you wish. If I do not manage to do it for you, I will give the sheet back to you and I will have no power over you."

Jiřík thanked the devil and was very grateful because he thought he might cheat the devil somehow. Much happier he went out of the room and walked to the Queen to please her. The Queen, seeing a smile on her darling's face, was also happier. They went for a walk together.

"Tell me, darling, what would please you to have?" Jiřík asked, hoping that he would get to know some task for the devil. He himself could not think up anything.

"I have everything. I only wish you were happier."

"I am happy again. Tell me something, we are only speaking. How would you like the castle decorated?"

"Our castle is nice enough at the front side but there is no outlook at the back side. If there was not the horrible rock, it would be better."

"You are right," Jiřík answered and decided immediately to assign the work to the devil. In the evening the devil stood in front

of the King and asked him what he wished to be done.

"I want you to remove the rock that shades our castle at the back."

"It will happen as you wish," the devil answered and left.

The King thought that the devil would not manage that and that he would have more time. Therefore he was scared when he got up in the morning and coming to the window saw a wide plain without a bit of the rock. He went for his wife and showed it to her.

"For God's sake, my husband, are you banded together with a devil, or are you a magician?" the Queen exclaimed and looked out of the window in wonder.

"I would do that much sooner. But I do not know myself what happened. Maybe some goblin listened to our conversation yesterday. Wish something else and we will see if it comes true!"

But the Queen was a clever woman. She knew that something was not right and that her husband held something terrible. For effect she said that she wished the whole plain turned into the most wonderful garden with flowers and plants and trees from all the countries of the world, all in blossom. But she thought to herself: "Wait, if this comes true until tomorrow, I will not give up until Jiřík confesses." In the evening the devil got the task to make the garden on the plain full of flowers and trees from all the countries of the world. He promised this and left. When the King woke up in the morning, the scent of a thousand flowers struck him that shone on the wide plain. It was a large paradise. The Queen who could not rest came too and with terror and pleasure she looked at the sweet flora. Suddenly she turned, took Jiřík's hand and spoke:

"Now, my dear husband, you cannot conceal any longer that you are banded together with a devil. I am sure of it. Tell me rather, for how long you are bound so that I can please you and give you good advice."

"It is late, my heart, today is the last day, he comes tonight for the last task and then I belong to him." After that Jiřík told her the whole history, who he was and what happened to him. The Queen forgave him gladly because she loved him very much and knew that he had erred out of love for her.

"Do not be afraid and moan so that no-one noticed it. We will be merry and when the devil comes in the evening, send him to me. I will think up something by that time."

Jiřík felt reborn and all the weight was off his mind. He joined his wife and was merry with his

children all day, as if nothing had happened. In the evening the devil came at his certain time. "What have you thought up today?" he asked the King.

"Go to my wife, she will tell you what she wishes. I do not know anything."

The devil entered the Queen's room. She was expecting him.

"You are the devil who should carry away my husband?"

"Yes."

"Can I choose one thing instead of him, be it anything?"

"Yes."

"And if you do not manage, he shall not be in your power any more?"

"He shall not."

"Very well. Come here and pull three hairs off my head. It must be neither more nor less and it mustn't hurt."

The devil frowned, came to her and quickly took three hairs and pulled them. But the lady cried anyway.

"You see, this is one mistake already, I told you that it should not hurt. Anyway, I pardon you. Now take the three hairs and measure them."

The devil measured them and the lady said: "Now you make the hairs longer by two feet each. But do not bind them, pull these so that each of them is two feet longer."

The devil looked at them for a while but he did not know what to do. He asked the Queen to let him take them to the hell and ask his journeymen for help. The Queen let him do so. The devil took the hairs and disappeared.

When he arrived at hell, he gathered all his journeymen, laid the hairs on the table in front of Satan and explained what had to be done with them.

"You lost this time, clever fellow," the lord said, "you met someone smarter. What to do with them? If we pull them, they will tear. If we hit them, they will break. If we put them into the fire, they will burn. There is nothing else to do other than to return and hand over not the hairs but the sheet."

"I will not go to her, it might be bad for me."

"Why do you not pay better attention? Now go and hand over what does not belong to you any longer."

The devil had to take the sheet and hand it over to whom it now beonged. He flew down to the castle but being afraid of entering he waited at the window until the King opened it. When he did so, the devil tossed the sheet into the room and disappeared. With utmost joy Jiřík picked up the sheet and ran to his wife who knew already how it all would finish. And they lived happily ever after.

THE FIRE BIRD AND RED FOX

by Karel Jaromír Erben

A King once had a huge beautiful garden. There were many rare trees. Yet the apple-tree which stood in the middle of it was the rarest. It grew one apple each day which was gold. It flowered in the morning, it grew during the day and it ripened by the night and the next day there was another one. However, no ripe apple survived until the next day, it was always lost during the night and nobody knew where and how. The King was very sad about this.

He once called his eldest son and said: "Go, my son, you will keep guard tonight. If you find out who takes those apples I will not save my treasures to reward you. If you manage to catch the thief, I will give you a half of my kingdom."

The prince tied a sword to his body, he took a crossbow and several arrows and he went to keep guard in the garden. There he sat under the apple-tree and waited. He had not been sitting for long when slumber came that he could not resist. His hands fell down in the grass, his eyes closed and the prince slept until white day as if he had been thrown in water. When he woke up in the morning, the apple was gone again.

"So have you seen the thief?" the King asked him.

"No-one came, the apple disappeared itself," the prince answered.

The King shook his head, he did not want to believe this. "Go and keep guard tonight, my son, and if you catch the thief, I will reward you richly," he said to his younger son.

The second prince armed himself as the first one had and went to keep guard. He fell asleep like his brother after some time. The apple was gone again when he woke up.

When his father asked him in the morning who had taken the apple, he answered: “Nobody, it disappeared itself.”

Then the youngest prince said: “Father, I will guard tonight to see if the apple also disappears.”

“My dear child,” the King told him, “I think you can do very little, you are too young and unwise. If the two elder ones have not managed to guard the golden apple then it will be even more difficult for you. Yet go if you want to.”

The youngest son went to the garden to guard in the evening when it was getting dark. He also took a sword, a crossbow and a few arrows as well as a hedgehog’s skin. He sat under the apple-tree, put this skin in his lap in case sleep came and his hands would fall. Then the skin would wake him up. At midnight a golden bird came, he sat on the tree and wanted to peck the apple away. At that moment one could hear the prince’ crossbow and an arrow hit the bird in the wing. The bird flew away but one of his feathers fell on the ground and the apple stayed on the tree.

“So, have you got the thief?” the King asked the next morning.

“No, I do not,” the prince replied. ”But all is not lost. I have a piece of his coat for the time being.”

He took out the golden feather and recounted what had happened to him. The King was very happy with the feather. It was very beautiful and it was shining so brightly that no more lights were necessary in the hall any

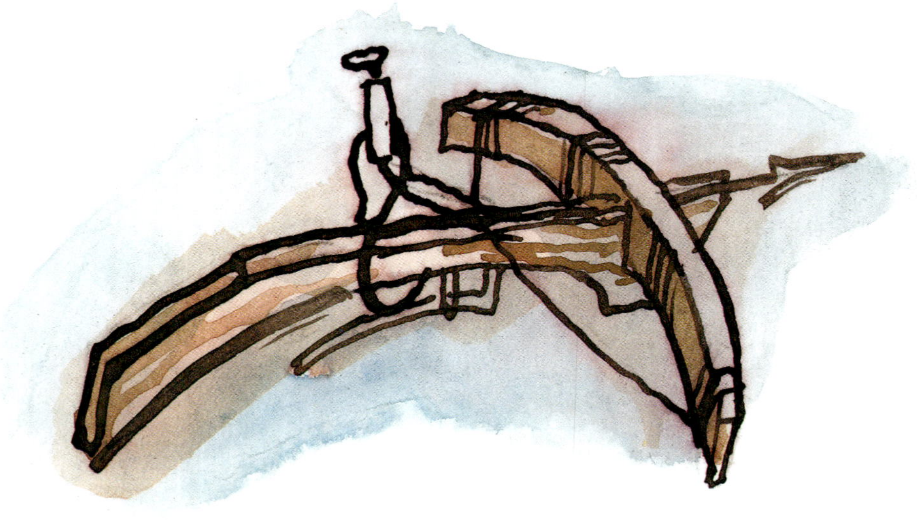

more. The courtiers who understood this said that that feather comes from Fire Bird and it is worth more than all the King's treasures.

Fire Bird did not come to the garden any more since that time and no more apples were lost. Yet they did not make the King happy any more. He kept thinking about Fire Bird. He was so very upset about not having him that his heart began to fade from this grief.

One day he called his three sons and said: "Dear children, you can see that I am becoming weaker every day. I am sure that if I heard Fire Bird's singing, my heart would recover. The one who will bring Fire Bird alive to me to sing, will immediately receive a half of the kingdom and will be my successor after my death."

The sons set out straight away. They said good-bye to their father and left to look for Fire Bird. They were not on their way for long when they arrived in a forest and there to a crossing.

"Which way will we take?" the eldest brother asked.

"There are three of us and there are three roads here," the second one answered, "let each of us take one of them if we go in three directions it will be easier to find Fire Bird."

"And who will take which one?" "You go whichever way you want, I will take the one which is left," the youngest brother said. The brothers were satisfied and each chose a way.

Then one of them said: "Let us leave a sign here so that the one who comes back soonest knows how the other two succeeded. Let each of us plant a twig in the ground. Whoever's twig grows will tell us that he found Fire Bird happily."

The brothers liked this idea. Each of them planted a twig next to his way and they left.

The eldest prince kept going his way until he arrived at a hill. He jumped off his horse, he left it to graze and sat on the grass. Then he took out his food and started to eat.

Red Fox came slowly: "Please, please lad, I am very hungry, give me something to eat."

As soon as the prince noticed her he took his crossbow and shot after her. Whether or not he missed her, she disappeared.

The same thing happened to the second brother. When he sat on a large meadow to eat something hungry Red Fox came and asked him for something to eat. As he shot after her, she disappeared from his sight.

The youngest brother kept going on until he arrived at a stream. He was hungry and tired so he jumped off his horse and

sat down on the grass on the bank to refresh himself.
When he started eating he also noticed Red Fox coming close and closer and then stopping not far away from him:

"Please, please, young lad, I am very hungry, let me have a bite of something, too."

The prince threw her a piece of sausage and said: "Come here and do not be afraid, Red Fox, I can see that you are more hungry than me and I have enough for both of us for today." Then he divided his food in two parts – one for himself, one for the fox.

Red Fox filled herself and then she said: "You fed me well, I will serve you well. Get on your horse and follow me. If you do what I tell you, Fire Bird will be yours."

Then she ran in front of him making way for him with her shaggy tail. She wiped away mountains, she filled the valleys, built bridges over water fords. The prince was trotting behind her when all of a sudden he found himself in front of a Copper Palace.

"Fire Bird is in this palace," Red Fox said, "go there at midday – the guards will be sleeping – and do not linger anywhere. You will find twelve black birds in golden cages in the first hall, twelve golden birds in wooden cages in the second one and Fire Bird will be sitting on a perch in the third hall. You will see two cages next to him – a golden one and a wooden one – but do not put him in the golden one, put him in the wooden cage otherwise it will go badly."

The prince entered

the Copper Palace and found everything as Red Fox had said. Fire Bird was sitting on a perch in the third hall as if he was sleeping. He was so beautiful that the prince' heart rejoiced. He took him and put him in the wooden cage, then he changed his mind and said: "How does such a lovely bird and such a shabby cage go together. Fire Bird belongs in a golden cage." So he took him from the wooden cage and put him in the golden one. But as soon as he closed him there, Fire Bird woke up and whistled. Suddenly a lot of whistling and croaking broke out from all the birds in the first two halls so that the people guarding the gate woke up. They ran in immediately, arrested the prince and took him to their King.

The King was very furious and said: "Who are you, thief, that you dared to cross so many guards to steal my Fire Bird?"

"I am no thief but I have come here to fetch the thief which you

harbour," the prince replied. "We have an apple-tree which bears golden apples in our royal garden back home. Only one apple a day flowered, grew and ripened and then your Fire Bird carried it away at night. And the King, my father, is seriously ill, his heart is fading and he will not get better until he hears your Fire Bird sing. And that is why I ask you to give him to me."

"You may have him," te King answered, "if you bring Golden Mane instead of him."

"Why did you not listen to me and why did you take the golden cage?" Red Fox was angry.

"I made a mistake indeed but do not be angry at me because of what happened. Tell me if you know something about Golden Mane."

"I do," Red Fox replied, "and I will help you once again. Get on your horse and follow me."

Again she ran first and she was making the way for him. Suddenly they appeared in front of a Silver Palace.

"Golden Mane is in this palace," Red Fox said. "Go there at midday when the guards will be sleeping and do not stop anywhere. You will find twelve black horses with golden curbs in the first stable, twelve white horses with black curbs in the second stable and Golden Mane will be standing next to his manger in the third stable. You will see two curbs next to him on the wall – a golden one and a leather one. But be careful, leave the golden one and give him the leather one. Otherwise it will not go well."

The prince went into the castle and found everything there as Red Fox had told him. Golden Mane was standing in the third stable and eat-ing fire from a silver manger. He was so beautiful that the prince could not take his eyes off him. Then he took the leather halter with black curb off the wall and gave it to Golden Mane. The horse stood there calm as a lamb. Suddenly he noticed a beautiful golden halter with a golden gem-studded curb. He liked it very much.

"How does that go together – such a beautiful horse and such a shabby curb?" So he took off the leather curb and replaced it with the golden one. As soon as the horse felt the golden curb, he reared and guffawed. So all the other horses in the first two stables started jumping and making noise and they woke the gatemen. These came running, arrested the prince and brought him before their King."

"Who are you, thief," the King accused him, "that you dared to cross so many guards to steal my Golden Mane?"

"I am no thief. I was not happy about getting your horse but I had to," the prince answered. And then he recounted how everything happened. He said that the King of the Copper Palace did not want to submit Fire Bird to him until be brought him Golden Mane. And then he asked to be given the horse.

"You can have him if you bring me maiden Goldilocks from the Golden Palace in the Black Sea," the King of the Silver Palace told him.

Red Fox was waiting for the prince out in the woods and when she saw he was coming without the horse she got very angry. "Have

I not told you to leave the golden curb on the wall and take the leather one? It is hard work with you. He who cannot be advised, cannot be helped either."

"Do not be angry with me, Red Fox, I did make a mistake indeed but please help me this time," the prince begged. "I will help you once more, for the last time. And if you obey me, then you can fix everything you have spoilt so unwisely. Sit on your horse and follow me."

Then she ran in front and made the way for him until they came

to the Golden Palace in the Black Sea. "The Sea Queen rules in this palace," Red Fox said. "She has three daughters and the youngest of them is Goldilocks. Go there and ask her to give you one of her daughters for a wife. When she tells you to choose one, take that who will be dressed in the most simple way."

The Sea Queen welcomed the prince warmly and when he told her why he was there she lead him to a room where her three daughters were sitting and spinning. They were so similar to each other that nobody in the world could have told them apart. And they were so beautiful that the prince had to hold his breath when he was looking in their eyes. Each of them had her head covered with a scarf so that one could not see their hair. Each of them was dressed differently. The first one had a scarf and a dress woven with gold and was using a golden reel. The second one was wearing a silver scarf and a dress woven by silver as well as a silver reel in her hand. The third daughter was dressed in a white scarf and dress and was spinning with and an ordinary reel.

"Choose the one you want," the Queen said and the prince pointed at the girl in white.

"Give me this one."

"Huh, huh. This is not your own idea, wait until tomorrow," the surprised Queen said.

The prince could not sleep from worrying how he would succeed the following day. As soon as dawn came he walked into the palace garden.

Once he stepped there the white girl appeared from nowhere: "Pay attention to a little fly circling around one of us if you want to recognise me today." Then she left just like she had come.

After noon the Queen led the prince back to the room where her daughters were. "If you recognise the one you chose yesterday, she is yours. If not you will lose your head."

The daughters were standing there one next to the other. They were all expensively and beautifully dressed and they all had golden hair which was shining so much that the prince' eyes were almost blinded. After a while his sight got used to it and he noticed a tiny gold fly circling around one of the maidens.

"This maiden belongs to me, she is the one I have chosen," he said. The Queen was surprised to see that he recognised her and said: "You will not get her so easily. You will have to accomplish a task I will give you tomorrow."

Then in the morning she showed him a big lake near the forest, she handed him a small golden sieve and said:

"If you manage to empty this lake with this sieve by tonight I will give you Goldilocks. You will lose your head if you do not."

The prince went sadly to the lake taking the sieve with him. He placed it in the water and took out some but as he took it out all the water ran out. Seeing he could not do anything, he sat on the wharf, put the sieve next to him and started thinking about what to do.

All of a sudden from nowhere the white maiden appeared again: "Why are you so upset?"

"Why should I be happy? I can see I will not get you because your mother gave me an impossible task," he replied. "Do not worry, all this can be done," the girl said. The she took the sieve and threw it in the middle of the lake. All the water began boiling and thick clouds began coming out of the lake and went to the ground so that one could not see three steps ahead.

At that moment the prince heard stamping and when he turned around he saw Red Fox and his horse behind her.

"Hurry, take the girl on the horse in front of you and ride away," she said to him.

The horse flew back like an arrow the way which Red Fox had made for him. She destroyed it with her shabby tail, she wiped away bridges, dug valleys, built mountains as it was all done before. The prince was happy that he had gained the golden-haired maiden but unhappy to exchange her for Golden Mane with the King of the Silver Palace.

The closer they were getting to this palace the slower he was riding and the sadder he became.

"You regret having to swap your beautiful Goldilocks for Golden Mane, don't you?" Red Fox spoke to him. "I have helped you win many things, I will not leave you now."

She jumped over a root and threw a somersault. And there was a second Goldilocks standing there instead of Red Fox. "Leave your maiden in the forest and take me to the King of the Silver Palace. Exchange me for Golden Mane together with the golden curb. Once you have him ride as quickly as you can with your girl."

The King was very happy about Goldilocks and he gave Golden

Mane together with the golden curb to the prince without delay.

Then he held a feast to honour the golden-haired maiden and invited all the noblemen.

After they had drunk a lot and were very gay, the King asked those nobles how they liked his golden-haired bride.

"Very beautiful, she could not be more beautiful but she seems to have fox' eyes," one of the nobles answered.

Once he pronounced that word, Goldilocks turned back into Red Fox in an instant, jumped out of the door and was gone. She destroyed her fox' road with her shabby tail behind her – she broke the bridges, dug valleys, built mountains, everything as it was before. When she caught up with them, they were near the Copper Palace with Fire Bird.

So she said to the prince: "How lovely Goldilocks and Golden Mane! Do you not regret giving Golden Mane for Fire Bird?"

"Of course I regret it because of Goldilocks," the prince replied, "but I do not regret it because of my father who will be well again."

Red Fox said to this: "Let Fire Bird be where Goldilocks and Golden Mane are. I have helped you on different occasions and I will help you on this one, too."

She jumped over a root in the forest, throwing a somersault. And a second Golden Mane stood there – he was exactly the same as the one Goldilocks was sitting on.

"Take me to the King of the Copper Palace to exchange me for Fire Bird. Once you have him ride quickly away," she said.

The King was very glad to have Golden Mane and he handed Fire Bird to the prince together with the golden cage without delay.

Then he invited many nobles, he was bragging about his horse Golden Mane and asked them how they liked him.

"Beautiful, he could not be more beautiful but he seems to have the tail of a fox," one of the nobles said.

As he pronounced that word Golden Mane turned back into Red Fox immediately, she jumped out of the gate and was gone. She ran after the prince and Goldilocks, she pulled down her fox' way. She caught up with them when they got to the stream where she had met the prince for the first time.

"Now you have Fire Bird, you have even more than you asked for so you do not need me any more. Ride home slowly and do not stop anywhere otherwise things will go badly for you," she said. Then she disappeared.

The prince was riding along his way. He had Fire Bird in the golden cage in one hand, Golden Mane with the golden curb next to him and the beautiful maiden

Goldilocks on this horse. When he arrived at the forest junction where he had parted with his brothers he remembered those branches each one had planted their way as a sign. The branches of the two brothers were dry but a lovely spreading tree grew from his one in the meantime. He rejoiced to see this and since both of them were very tired after such a long journey, he wanted them to have a rest under that tree.

He got off his horse and helped the golden-haired maiden off Golden Mane. Then he tied both the horses to a tree and hung the cage with Fire Bird on a branch. Before long they fell asleep.

While they were sleeping his brothers came back each from his side. Both of them were empty-handed and they met there at the same moment. They saw their dry branches as well as the lovely spreading tree of the youngest brother. They also saw their brother sleeping under this tree with a beautiful golden-haired maiden next to him and they saw Golden Mane and Fire Bird in the cage above them, too.

At that moment horrible thoughts came to their minds and one of them said to the other: "Our brother will now receive half of the kingdom from our father and he will be his successor after his death. It will be better to kill him. You will take the golden-haired maiden, I will take Golden Mane and we will give Fire Bird to our father to sing for him. We will part the kingdom equally."

They did what they had decided. They cut their brother's body into many pieces and they threatened the golden-haired maiden with death if she told the truth.

After their arrival home they placed Golden Mane in a marble stable, they put Fire Bird in the cage in the room where the King was lying and they supplied the golden-haired maiden with a beautiful room and many girls to serve her.

The old ill King looked at Fire Bird and asked his sons if they

had any news about their youngest brother.

"We have not heard of him. He might have died on his way," the brothers answered. Their father stayed low-spirited, Fire Bird did not sing, Golden Mane kept his head down and Goldilocks did not say a word, she did not brush her golden hair and kept on crying.

While the prince was lying chopped in the woods, Red Fox came to him. She took all the pieces put them together as they belonged. She would have brought him to life but she was not able to.

But then she noticed a crow with two baby crows flying above the body. She hid under a bush in the grass.

When one of the young ones sat on the body to eat it, Red Fox jumped out and caught it by the wing pretending she wanted to tear it.

The old crow came closer as she was afraid. She sat on a bush and told Red Fox: "Leave my poor child, it did not harm you in any way. I will serve you when you need it."

"I need it now," Red Fox said. "If you bring me live and dead water from the Black Sea, I will let your baby live." The crow promised she would bring it and flew away.

She flew for three days and three nights and she came back with two fish bladders full of water. There was live water in one of them and dead water in the other one. Red Fox took the bladders and tore the young crow in two pieces.

Then she put the two halves back together, sprinkled it with dead water and they grew back together. Then she sprinkled it with the live water and the crow moved its wings and flew away. Then she sprinkled prince' chopped body with the dead water. It was whole again, even without scars. When she sprinkled it with live water, the prince woke up as if he was dreaming, he got up and said: "Oh, how deep was I sleeping."

"Oh yes, very deep. And if it was not for me, you would never ever have woken up again. Had I not warned you not to stop and to go home directly?" Red Fox said.

Then she recounted to him what had happened. She walked with him to the side of the forest not far away from his father's palace. She gave him a simple dress, said good-bye to him and disappeared.

The prince went to the palace and started working in the horse stables. Nobody recognized him.

Once he heard two henchmen talking: "It is a pity that the beautiful Golden Mane keeps his head down and does not want to eat."

"Give me some peas. I want to bet you that he will eat again," the prince told them.

"Huh, huh, even our ploughing horses do not eat such rubbish," the henchmen laughed.

But the prince put a bit of peas in the horse' marble manger, stroked his golden mane and told him: "Why are you so sad, my dear Golden Mane?"

The horse recognized his master by the voice, he jumped up, he snorted, guffawed and started eating peas.

This information spread round the whole palace quickly. Even the King heard that one of his henchmen had healed Golden Mane. The King had him called and said to him: "I hear that you helped Golden Mane. I wish you could help Fire Bird, too, so that he would sing. He is sad, his wings are down and he does not want to eat anything. If he dies, I will die, too."

"Do not be afraid, my King, he will not die," the prince said. "Order someone to bring some barley and he will surely eat, he will be happy and sing again."

"Huh, huh," laughed the servants who fetched the barley. "He feeds Fire Bird with barley which even our geese do not want to eat."

They had to bring the barley, the prince sprinkled some in the golden cage. Then he stroked his golden feathers and said: "Why are you so sad, my Fire Bird?"

The bird recognized his voice, shook himself, arranged his wings, started jumping and eating and then he sang so beautifully the old king's ill heart recovered. And after Fire Bird sang for the second and third time, the King felt so strong that he got up and hugged the unknown henchman out of happiness.

Then the King said: "What shall we do with that beautiful golden-haired maiden whom my sons brought with them? She does not speak, she does not brush her golden hair, does not eat anything and keeps on crying."

"Allow me, my King, to have a word with her. She might become happy," the henchman said. The King led him to her, the prince took her white hand and said: "Why are you so sad, my bride?"

The girl recognized him immediately, she cried of joy and hugged him. The King wondered why he called her his bride and that she hugged him. The prince told him: "Do you not know, my royal father, your youngest son?

It was not my brothers who acquired Fire Bird, Golden Mane and this pretty Goldilocks."

And then he recounted how everything had happened. The girl witnessed that his brothers threatened her with death if she told what they had done. The brothers were standing there seeing that they had been discovered and they were trembling as an aspen leaf and they could not say a word. The King became furious and had both of them executed immediately. Then the prince married the pretty Goldilocks, he got a half of the kingdom and the second half after his father's death.

Long, Broad and Sharp Eyes

by Karel Jaromír Erben

Once there was a King who was already old and had but one son. One day he called the son to him and told him: "My dear son, you know well that the ripe fruits fall to make space for other fruits. My head is also ripening. Maybe the sun will not shine long upon it. Before you bury me, I would like to see my future daughter, your wife. Marry, my son!"

The Prince said: "I would like, father, to follow your will. But I do not have a bride, I do not know any."

So the old King put his hand into his pocket, took out a golden key and handed it to the son: "Go up the tower, to the highest floor. Look round there and then tell me which one you would like."

The Prince did not tarry and left. He has never been upstairs and he also had not heard what could be there.

When he came up to the last floor, he saw a small iron door in the ceiling that seemed to be a trapdoor. It was locked. He opened it with the golden key, lifted it and entered upstairs above them. There was a large round hall, the ceiling was blue as a sky in a clear night and silver stars glittered on it. The floor was covered with a green silky carpet. Around the hall there were twelve high windows in golden frames in the walls. In each window on the crystal glass

there was a maiden portrayed with rainbow colours. Each one had a royal crown. In each window there was a different one dressed in a different way. They were so fair that the Prince was amazed by the sight of them. As he looked at them in wonder not knowing which one to choose, the maidens started to move as if alive. They turned to him, smiled – it seemed that they would start to speak any minute.

Suddenly the Prince noticed that one of the twelve windows was covered with a white cloth. He removed the cloth to have a look at what was under it. There was a maiden dressed in white, girded with a silver belt, with a pearl crown on her head. She was the most beautiful one but sad and pale as if she rose from the dead.

The Prince stood long before the painting as if struck. As he looked at it his heart started to pain and he said: "I want to have this one and no-one else!" As he said the word, the maiden bent her head and blushed as a rose. At that moment all the paintings disappeared.

When he came down again after a while and told his father what he had seen and which maiden he had chosen, the old King saddened, began to think and said: "You did badly, my son, that you uncovered what had been covered. You threw yourself in a great danger through it. This maiden is under the power of an evil sorcerer, captured in the Iron Castle. Whoever tried to rescue her, did not return. Yet what has happened cannot be undone. The given word is a law. Go, try out your luck and come healthy back home to me!"

The Prince parted with his father, mounted a horse and went for the bride. He was to go through a large forest. He went on and on until he was lost.

As he strayed in bushes, among rocks and moors with his horse not knowing where to go, he heard somebody crying behind him: "Hey, wait for me!"

The Prince looked back and saw a tall man hurrying after him.

"Wait and take me with you. If you take me into service, you will not regret it."

"Who are you," the Prince said, "and what can you do?"

"My name is Long and I can stretch. Do you see the bird's nest there on the high fir? I can take it down and you needn't climb up."

Long started to stretch, his body grew rapidly until he was as tall as the fir. He reached the nest and shrunk in a moment again and handed it to the prince.

"You know your performance well. But what is the use of the nest when you cannot lead me out of the forest!"

"Well, it is an easy thing," Long said and started to stretch again until he was three times taller than the highest fir in the forest. He looked round and said: "The shortest way from the forest is in this direction."

Then he shrunk, took the horse bridle and went ahead. Before long they were behind the forest. A wide plain was in front of them and behind the plain there were high grey rocks like walls of a large city, and mountains covered with forest.

"Over there, my lord, comes my friend," Long said and pointed to the side on the plain. "You should also employ him. Truly, he would serve you well."

"Shout to him and call him, I will see who he is."

"It is a bit too far, my lord," Long said. "He would hardly hear me and it would take him long to come because he has much to carry. I would rather fetch him."

Again Long stretched so high that his head disappeared in the clouds, made two three steps, took his friend on his shoulders and put him on the ground in front of the prince. He was a stout man with a stomach that would incorporate four buckets. "Who are you," the Prince asked him, "and what can you do?"

"My name, oh lord, is Broad and I can widen."

"Show it to me, then."

"Lord, flee fast! Fast back towards the forest!" Broad cried and began to swell.

The Prince did not understand why he should flee. Yet seeing that Long paced back toward the forest, he spurred his horse and galloped after him. It was high time to do so, otherwise Broad would crush him and his horse with his stomach that grew rapidly. Suddenly he was everywhere as if a mountain rolled up there. After that Broad ceased to swell, he puffed that the forests bent and became as he had been before.

"You have made me run!" the Prince said to him. "But I do not find such a fellow every day. Come along with me."

And so they went on. When they came close to the rocks, they met a man who had his eyes tied up with a handkerchief.

"Oh lord, this is our third friend," Long said. "You should employ him, too. Truly it would not be in vain."

"Who are you," the Prince asked. "Why have you your eyes tied up? You do not see the way indeed?"

"Oh lord, on the contrary. I see too much and that is why I

have to tie up my eyes. I see with the tied up eyes as the others do with the untied eyes. When I untie them, I see all through everything. When I look at something sharply I set fire to it and what cannot burn breaks into pieces. That is why my name is Sharp Eyes."

Then he turned to the opposite rock, untied the kerchief and focused his fiery eyes on it. The rock began to crack and the pieces flew from it to all sides. In a short while there was nothing left but a heap of sand. Something like fire glittered in it. Sharp Eyes went there and brought it to the Prince. It was pure gold.

"Wow, what an inestimable fellow you are!" the Prince said. "Only a fool would not want to use your service. But as you have such good sight, have a look and tell me if it is far to the Iron Castle and what is happening there."

"If you went alone, lord," Sharp Eyes said, "you may not reach the place in a year. But with us you will get there even today. They are just preparing a dinner for us."

"And what does my bride do?"

"In a small chamber
In a high tower
A sorcerer guards her."

And the Prince said: "You who are good, help me rescue her!"

And they all promised to help him. So they led him among the grey rocks through the chasm that Sharp Eyes made in them with his eyes, and through the rocks, high mountains and deep forests further and further. If there was an obstacle on the way, the three fellows removed it quickly. When the sun was coming down to the west, the mountains began to descend and the forests began to thin and the rocks hid among heather. And when the sun was already above the west, the Prince saw the Iron Castle not far ahead. When the sun was setting, he went on the iron bridge and entered the gate. As soon as the sun was set, the iron bridge rose itself, the gates closed at once and the prince with the fellows were captured in the Iron Castle.

After they looked round the courtyard, the prince led his horse to the stable – everything was ready – and they went to the castle. In the courtyard, in the stable, in the castle hall and in chambers they saw through the dusk many people richly dressed, both lords and servants. None of them moved, they were all petrified. They went through several chambers and came to the dining room. It was clearly lit, a table stood in the middle, many tasty meals and drinks aplenty lay on it, and the table was laid for four persons. They waited and waited because they thought that somebody would come. When nobody came after long, they sat and drank to their hearts' content.

When they finished, they started to look for a place to sleep. All of a sudden, the door opened quickly and the sorcerer entered. He was an old bent man in a long black dress, with a bald head and a grey beard to his knees. Instead of a belt he had three hoops. By the hand he led a fair, a very fair maiden dressed in white. She had a silver belt on her waist and a pearl crown

on her head but she was pale and sad, as if she rose from the dead. The Prince recognized her immediately, leapt and went to meet her.

Yet before he could speak a word, the sorcerer spoke: "I know why you have come. You want to lead this Queen away from here. May it happen, take her if you can guard her for three nights so that she does not flee. If she flees from you, you and your servants will petrify as those had who have come before you."

Then he indicated the Queen to sit on the sofa and left. The Prince could not take his eyes off her, so beautiful she was. He started to talk to her, he asked various things. But she did not answer, did not smile or look at anyone as if she was made of marble. So he sat next to her and intended not to fall asleep the whole night nor let her flee. To make sure Long stretched as a belt and snaked round the whole chamber along the walls. Broad sat in the door, swelled and clogged it up so that a mouse could not slip in. Sharp Eyes stood at the column the middle of the room to keep guard. In a short while they all started to slumber, fell asleep and slept the whole night like logs.

The Prince woke first when dawn began. But he felt as if someone had thrust a dagger in his heart: the Queen had gone away. He woke his servants immediately and asked them what to do.

"Do no be afraid, lord," Sharp Eyes said and looked sharply out of the window. "I see her already! There is a forest one hundred miles far from here, in the middle of the forest there is an old oak and on the top of the oak there is an acorn. The acorn is her. Let Long take me on his shoulders and we will get her."

Long lifted him immediately, he stretched and went and one step was ten miles. Sharp Eyes showed him the way.

Before one could run round a house they were back and Long handed the acorn to the Prince: "Lord, drop it on the floor!"

The Prince dropped it and at that moment the Queen stood by him. When the sun started to show behind the mountains the door opened noisily. The sorcerer entered the chamber and smiled slyly. But when he saw the Queen, he frowned, murmured and crash! One iron hoop broke and rebound. He took the maiden by the hand and led her away.

The Prince had nothing to do for the whole day but walk in the castle and around the castle and look at what was strange.

It seemed that the life had vanished everywhere in one moment. In one chamber he saw some prince holding a poised dagger with both hands as if he wanted to cut somebody in halves. Yet the swipe did not reach its target, he petrified. In one chamber there was a petrified knight as if he was escaping terrified from someone. And tripping over the doorsill, he fell but did not reach the ground. Under a chimney some servant sat, held a piece of roast from dinner in one hand and carried a mouthful with the other one but he did not reach his mouth: just at the mouth he was to petrify, too. And he saw many other petrified ones, everybody in the position of how he was when the sorcerer said: "Petrify!" And he saw many beautiful petrified horses, too. Everything was deserted and dead in the castle and around the castle. There were trees but without leaves. There were meadows but without grass. There was a river but it did not flow. There were no birds the singers, not a violet the daughter of the land, not a little fish.

The Prince with his fellows found a tasty and plentiful feast in the morning, at noon and in the evening. The meals carried itself and the wine poured itself. After dinner the door opened again and the sorcerer brought the Queen to the Prince to guard her. Despite all of them deciding that they would resist falling asleep in all possible ways it was in vain and they fell asleep again.

When the Prince woke up at dawn and saw that the Queen had disappeared, he jumped and pulled the shoulder of Sharp Eyes: "Hey, get up, you Sharp Eyes! Do you know where the Queen is?"

He rubbed his eyes, had a look and said: "I see her already! There is a mountain two hundred miles far from here and in the mountain there is a rock and in the rock there is a precious stone. The stone is her. If Long takes me there, we will get her."

Long took him on his shoulders, he stretched and went and one step was twenty miles. Sharp Eyes focused his fiery eyes on the rock and the rock went to thousand pieces. Among them the precious stone glittered. They took it and brought it to the prince. He dropped it again and the Queen stood there once more. When the sorcerer came after a while and led her away, his eyes glittered with anger and crack!

Another iron hoop broke and flew astray.

That day everything was the same as yesterday. After dinner the sorcerer brought the Queen again, looked sharply into the Prince' eyes and remarked derisively: "We shall see who is the stronger one, if you shall win, or me!" He left with these words.

They tried even harder to resist sleep. They did not want even to sit. They wanted to walk the whole night but it was in vain. Finally it happened, they fell asleep walking one after another and the Queen fled for all that.

The Prince woke up first in the morning. When he did not see the Queen, he woke Sharp Eyes.

"Hey, get up, Sharp Eyes. Have a look where the Queen is!"

Sharp Eyes looked long to the distance. "Oh lord," he said. "She is far, very far! There is a Black Sea three hundred miles far from here and in the middle on the seabed there lies a shell and in the shell there is a golden ring. The golden ring is her. Yet do not be afraid, we will get her despite all that! However, Long must take Broad with us today, we will need him!"

Long took Sharp Eyes on one shoulder and Broad on the other one, he stretched and went and one step was thirty miles. When they came to the Black Sea, Sharp Eyes showed him from where he should lift the shell. Long stretched his hand as much as he could but he could not reach the seabed yet.

"Wait, friends, wait a little while, I will help you," Broad said and swelled as much as his stomach could. Then he got down to the shore and drank. In a short while the water subsided so much that Long could easily reach the seabed and take the shell out of the sea. He took the ring from it, lifted his friends on his shoulders and hurried back. But it was a bit difficult to run with Broad on his shoulder as he had water from half of the sea in him. So Long shook him off to the ground in one wide valley. It banged as if bellows fell from a tower. The whole valley was under water like a lake at once. Broad could hardly get out of it.

Meanwhile, the Prince felt already worried in the castle. The sun shine started to show behind the mountains and the servants were not back. The more fiery rays came out, the greater was his dread. Soon a thin strip of the sun showed in the east. Suddenly the door opened with a strong bang. The sorcerer stood at the doorway and looked round the chamber.

When he saw that the Queen was not there, he guffawed hideously and entered the chamber. But suddenly ting! The window went to pieces, the golden ring fell on the floor and the Queen stood there at that moment again.

Sharp Eyes had seen what was happening in the castle and in what danger their lord was and told Long. Long had made a step and thrown the ring to the chamber through the window. The sorcerer cried with anger so that the castle shook. And crack! The third hoop broke on him and flew astray. The sorcerer changed into a raven and flew away through the broken window.

Then the fair maiden spoke and thanked the Prince for rescuing her and blushed as a rose. All of a sudden, everything revived in the castle. The one who held the poised dagger swished it through the air and tucked it into the scabbard. The one who tripped over the doorsill fell on the ground but arose immediately and touched his nose to find out if it was complete. The one, who sat under the chimney, put the mouthful of the roast into his mouth and went on eating. And so everybody finished what he had started and where he or she had stopped. The horses stamped and neighed in the stables. The trees round the castle turned green as a periwinkle. There were plenty of pied flowers on the meadows and high in the sky a lark twittered. In the speedy river shoals of tiny fish glided and everything was so alive, so merry!

Meanwhile, many lords gathered in the chamber where the Prince was. All thanked him for their deliverance. But he said: "Do not thank me. I would be what you have been but for my faithful servants Long, Broad and Sharp Eyes."

And soon after that he set forth on the way home to his father, the old King. He went with his bride and with his servants Long and Sharp Eyes and all the lords accompanied him. On their way they met Broad and took him with them.

The old King wept with joy that his son had been so lucky. He had thought that the Prince would never come back. Soon the noisy wedding took place. It lasted three weeks and all the lords whom the Prince had rescued were invited.

When it was after the wedding, Long, Broad and Sharp Eyes announced to the young King that they would go to the world to seek work. The young King reasoned with them and asked them to stay: "I will give you everything that you would need until your death, you needn't do anything!" But they did not like such an idle living, asked him for pardon and went. They have been wandering in the world until today.

The Princess with a Golden Star on her Forehead

by Božena Němcová

There once lived a King and a Queen and the Queen had a golden star on her forehead. They loved each other but their happiness did not last long. It is not possible to describe the King's grief, it is known only to those who have lost what they had loved.

For a long time the King did not want even to look at the child that had been the cause of its mother's death. At last the father's love won and the smile of the beloved child bound him by an eternal tie. She was a child so lovely, a living picture of her beautiful mother, that everyone's eye stayed bound to her. Thanks to her exceptional loveliness the girl was called Lada.

A few years passed from the time when the Queen had died. Courtiers forced the King to remarry for he would become more calm and merry. He answered them in this manner: "When the Queen lay on her death bed and was parting from me, she asked me not to marry any woman that would not wholly resemble her. I swore to that and took gods for witnesses. I will therefore seek a woman that will wholly resemble her. If I do not find such a one, I will never marry." The courtiers agreed with him. After this was concluded the King set out on a journey.

He entrusted Lada, the bud in bloom, to careful nurses, his land to a devoted warden and left with numerous folk to seek his bride. He went through principalities, kingdoms, he went through half the world and he saw virgins with angel-like faces. But still there was none with a golden star on her forehead, none resembled the dead lady. Sadly he went home. There was Lada running to meet him and welcome him warmheartedly after the long journey. The King was overwhelmed by the mature lady. It was her. She was the woman whom he loved above all, her eyes, hair, body, the glittering golden star on her forehead. Lada, her daughter, had all that.

"Alas, alas," the King thought. When he saw the image of his wife, all memories of his wife and past fortune awoke in him and he felt hopeless. Finally he decided in his desperate state that he marry Lada. He wanted to resist the high hills that nature put between him and his daughter in this sense. So he went to his daughter and revealed her the thought of her dead mother. Lada was shocked but she pretended to take her father's suggestion as a joke. After a short contemplation she said: "I will marry you, dear father, if you buy me a dress sewn from gold-crest wings."

"I will, my darling, I will buy you anything you wish. Only fulfil my plea," the King answered. He announced that he would give much money to any person who brought such a dress. What won't people do for money? Within a few days the dress was in the castle. The King brought it to the daughter. She did not know what to think up to prolong the time and thus gave her father another idea. She ordered another dress, this time of sunny colour. And again it was announced by the King and he got such a dress. When he brought it to Lada, she said: "Buy me one more dress, father, this time of heavenly colour, decorated with stars. After that I will marry you."

What would the King not give to her! Messengers ran in all directions and tailors tried hard to devise the dress of heavenly pattern, decorated with stars. But what won't the human mind devise when so much money is concerned! Even such a dress was sewn, only big diamonds replaced stars. There was nothing for it. Lada had to promise her father. But she worried about it and wept. That night she had a dream. A beautiful lady stood in front of her who had a golden star on her forehead. She put a white veil, as light as breath, on the bed, and said: "Lada, I am your mother. I know what is happening here. Your own father wants to marry you. It mustn't happen. I have come to help you. Have a simple dress sewn tomorrow, put this veil woven from fog over your head and escape. As long as you have it on, nobody will see you. Do not care about your father, I will reveal myself to him and give him inspiration." After these words Lada felt a light breath on her cheek and her mother disappeared. She found the veil in the morning and hid it quickly. Then she ordered her maid to have a coat of mice' fur made reaching to her heels. The maid thinking that it must be for some amusement, did not tell anybody and ordered the fur-coat herself. When it was ready, she brought it to the princess. The wedding was to be on the third day. There was hustle and bustle in the castle and the King was full of pleasure. Only the bride did not think about marriage. As soon as she had the fur-coat, she put it on, tied up the three dresses, put the wimple on her head and the veil on her face and dressed this way parted from the father's castle. She went into the wide world in tears. She walked far without knowing where to turn. Then she came to a town that was very beautiful. Just at the edge on the hill stood a King's castle. Lada decided to enter it and ask for work. But she did not want to take the bundle with her. Not far from the castle there was a pine-wood and a spring by it. Lada picked up a stone at the spring and put the bundle and the veil under it. A fish peeped out of the spring.

"Do not tell anyone, little fish, and look after it carefully," Lada asked the fish and and then went to the castle. She dusted her face with ashes on the way, frowned her forehead and lowered her wimple. If you imagine her mice-coat that she was almost all wrapped in, who would look for beauty in her? The servants burst into loud laughter when seeing the ugly maid and sent her away. But she asked so urgently to receive work in the kitchen that a cook took pity on her and allowed her into the kitchen. He forbade her sternly to show herself to the lordship otherwise he would be punished for taking such a girl into service. Lada was pleased that she had got work where she would be protected from all pursuit and nobody would notice her. She judged well. Nobody looked at her at all.

The land where this happened belonged to a King who had an only son, Hostivít. He was a noble youth, very reliable. All serfs looked forward to the time when the prince would be the King. It would be a wonderful time. The King was old and he would like Hostivít to have chosen a princess already. But he did not desire that. The kitchen

miss, too, heard the praise of the prince from the the rest of the servants. She would like to see the famous lord. Once she had the opportunity. She was alone in the kitchen when the prince passed by. She ran out and looked at him. We will see further if she liked him.

It was the King's anniversary. Guests gathered from distant countries to visit the wonderful feast and joy that lasted for three days. Lada was pondering the whole day. When the evening came, she asked the cook to let her look at the guests who she had never seen.

"Oh you lazy girl, you want to poke your nose among lords so that someone will see you and wonder what kind of servants there are in the castle?"

"Do not be afraid, master, that I will cross somebody's way. I will hide in a corner where nobody notices me." The cook did not want to, he did not, but then he murmured something about inquisitiveness and let the kitchen miss have a look. Lada went directly to the spring, picked up the stone and took the dress out of the bundle that was sewn from the gold-crest wings. Then she took off her wimple and the mice-coat, she washed her face, smoothed her hair and dressed herself in the pretty clothes. Of course she did not wish to see lordship, she wished

to dance with the handsome prince and speak with him. When she was dressed, she put the veil over her eyes and hurried to the castle. First she smoothed her dress in front of the mirror, then she entered the dancing hall, stood among the guests and stripped the veil from her forehead. Everybody turned to her at once but nobody knew who she was and where she had come from. Hostivít who had been flying from one lady to another as a playful butterfly, came to her first of all. As soon as he saw the noble face of the strange lady, he felt that his freedom had faded for ever.

"Who are you, fair lady, that I can remember neither your face nor your name?" Hostivít asked Lada.

"Trust in your hospitality brought me here to have entertainment. If you like to see me, do not want to know who I am," Lada answered with such a pleading look that Hostivít did not dare to ask any more.

Music started to play, everybody went for his lady. Even the prince stood in the row with his dancer who was not to be equalled. Time passed by quickly though he wanted it to be hundred times longer. The night started to draw in and the princess thanked her host, wishing to leave. The prince asked for a few more minutes but she would not stay a moment. She only promised that she would come again the next day. She quickly ran through the castle, reached the spring and took off the dress. It was high time to appear in the kitchen again. When she was leaving, the little fish peeped out of the spring again and Lada asked her to look after them. All the servants were asleep, nobody noticed when the kitchen miss came.

Every morning a valet announced what should be prepared for prince' breakfast. But that day he came saying that the prince did not know himelf what to order. They should prepare anything. "I do not know what has happened to the lord," the valet added, "I have not seen him so merry. He sings dancing from one room to another, and when I ask him this or that he says: 'Do what you want.'"

"Kind person," the cook answered, "maybe he liked some princess yesterday and he remembers her today."

"You are right, old man, there was one lady, but nobody knows who she is. He spent the whole evening with her."

The kitchen miss was cleaning something, and she leaned her head deep so that nobody would notice how she flushed. She pretended not to care about the valet's speech but she did not miss a single word. She would do the best things imaginable for the cook because she wanted him to let her look at the guests again in the evening. He promised this gladly.

When she had done all her work, she ran to the spring, took off the mice-coat, put on the sunny dress, put the veil over her head and hurried to the castle. The dance had already started. The prince did not speak the whole evening, he only looked to the door and waited for the moment when a servant opened them. Before long, his beautiful unknown lady stood in front of the hall, similar to the goddess whose name she bore. And again the prince stricken with love was happy. The ladies envied Lada her beauty and wonderful dress and gentlemen envied the prince her favour. This night Lada was delayed a bit because she could not resist the request of the handsome man whom she loved as deeply as he did her. It was dark when she came to the spring. She quickly took off her dress, dusted her face and ran like the wind to the castle where everything was alarmed.

"I do not like it, next time you will not go anywhere," the cook grumbled when she entered the kitchen. But she asked for pardon and started to work as busy as a bee. The cook was an old, good

man, and when he saw how hard she worked, he forgot his anger. Again the valet entered the kitchen. When the cook asked what the prince would order for breakfast, the valet answered that the prince would not eat anything. He sits in the armchair, eyes closed, and when somebody asks him, he is as silent as the grave. "I do not know," he finished his news, "the lady who visited us twice perhaps cast a spell on him."

"You, kitchen miss, what do you think about it, you also had a look, did you see the foreign lady?" the cook called to Lada who rotated the grill.

"Of course I did. But I do not understand if she is beautiful. I liked her and so did probably the prince because he spoke with her all the time," answered the kitchen miss to the cook. But if she did not stand at the grill, he would see her cheek that flushed as fire under the dust.

Due to her diligence for the whole day Lada got permission from the cook to go to the ball again. This time at the spring she put on the dress of the heavenly colour, decorated with stars. Nobody could see her because of the glitter and the pinewood was lit by the light that radiated from her

so much that she saw herself in the spring. She went to the castle with a worried heart this time. She had to say good-bye to her darling. She could surely say who she was. But she was afraid of her father's revenge and that he would want her back. That is why she decided to keep silent until she had discovered her father's plans and knew if he had already forgotten her.

Hostivít was out of his senses. He enjoyed nothing. Even the old King looked at the door expecting the beautiful magic lady to enter and hoping for a merry face on his son.

"Why are you so sad?" a melodious voice sang next to Hostivít. Lada like a morning star stood next to him and one ray from her eye cleared the frowning face of her darling. The old King and many guests gathered round her, welcomed her and could not let their eyes stray from such a beauty. That night neither Lada nor the prince could dance. They walked from one room to another and spoke about their love silently. The closer morning was, the sadder they became. The last hall shone with white marble and it was surrounded by sweet-smelling flowers and trees. One could think that he had entered a conservatory. There Lada and Hostivít sat on a sofa and tears shimmered in their eyes.

"My dear Lada, my only love, stay with me and be my wife," the prince begged with such a moving voice that its sound got through poor Lada's soul with unknown bliss.

"Do not beg me so, you make my heart heavy. You know that I

cannot fulfil your plea yet. Be assured of my deep love. Take this ring with which I betroth you for ever."

Hostivít took the precious ring with warm thanks. Then he took his own ring with diamonds off his finger and presented it to Lada.

"We are betrothed now," she said. "I am yours, you are mine. He who brings it back to you, believe him. He will be a messenger who will declare our upcoming meeting."

A short while passed in kisses and sweet dialogues and then Lada disappeared. In vain Hostivít ran to the hall where she had left. In vain he wailed as a hopeless empty man. Lada did not come back and he did not know where he should seek her.

With a heavy heart and in tears the girl stripped off the glittering dress in the pinewood, put it under the stone, asked the little fish to care for it and hurried to the kitchen in her mice-coat. The ring of the engagement was hidden at her breast.

When she came to the castle, people were running wildly, and prince' chamberlains almost broke their legs with their hurrying up and down the stairs. Lada asked in the kitchen what had happened.

"You spend nights outside and in the morning you sleep when walking," the cook scolded her. "Have you not heard that the prince is deadly ill? A devil brought the magic lady to us. Poor, poor lord! I am so worried that I do not know what to do with my hands."

Lada was stricken. She did not know if she should go to Hostivít or what else she could do. Then a servant to came her with some spices and ordered her to cook something for the prince. Lada pulled it from his hands and she stood at the fireplace at once. The servant ran away, and so did the cook. Before he came back, Lada had the spices in a pot and wanted to carry it upstairs.

"What are you doing? Could you not call somebody or wait for me? If the King saw you in your fur-coat, he would sicken."

"Oh, do not be afraid, master, he will not see me. I will do the work for you and carry it upstairs," Lada offered willingly. "I will give it to a chamberlain."

On her way she took the ring from her bosom and put it into the pot. She put the pot on a table in the room and ran downstairs hoping that the prince would calm down. At the same time she decided that she does not confess if the prince asked how the ring got into the soup. And it came to this in a short while.

As soon as the prince drank the spices and saw the ring on the bottom, he alarmed the whole castle. The question if he poured the soup into the pot, was the concern of the cook. The cook believed that a mouse hair had got into the

spices. He did not want to be shamed and asked for pardon and said that the kitchen miss did the work when he was busy. The kitchen miss had to go to the prince. She hesi-tated enough and she did not want to go but the servants took her and led her to the prince' chamber. As soon as she entered, she knelt on the floor and bowed her head so that prince would not see her body and recognize her face.

"It was you who put the ring into the pot?" the prince asked being fully awake. He observed the kneeling kitchen miss carefully.

"Oh merciful lord!" Lada said with a changed voice. "I poured the spices into the pot but I do not know anything of the ring. If it was there, somebody had to put it in accidentally."

Lada spoke steadily and the prince released her when he could not make her confess. Lada was glad that she had escaped, thanked him and hurried to the kitchen where she had to tell everything to the cook. But regardless of her ugly furcoat, the prince observed her noble body when she was leaving, he noticed her beautiful step and tiny feet that a clumsy kitchen miss usually did not have. He kept speculating how he could see her without being noticed.

It was a habit in that town that the people, both the poor and the rich, liked to bath. There were two baths, one was royal, the other for home servants. Twice a week everybody bathed in it. The bath came to Hostivít's mind at first. This was the best possibility of how to detect the strange kitchen miss. It was exactly the day of the bath. The prince went into the garden secretly and headed to the women's bath. There he made three eye-size holes in the wall and went back to his chamber. Doctors thanked God that he walked already after being so near to death. Hostivít pleased them by saying that the magic spices had healed him. This gratified them greatly.

In the evening, at the bathing time, the prince stole from the castle into the garden, went to the bath and hid in the thick bushes where nobody noticed him. All the women bathed first and the last one was the kitchen miss because no woman wanted to bath with her. The kitchen miss was grateful for this. When the prince saw the kitchen miss, he came nearer to the wall and hardly breathed.

Lada entered the bath in thoughts. When she had locked the door after her, she took off the mice-coat and stood there in

a simple skirt. Hostivít's cheeks blushed when he saw the comely body. A blissful feeling overcame his heart. But when the kitchen miss took off her wimple, washed her face and a star glittered on her forehead, the prince could not collect himself any longer and cried: "Oh Lada, my dear Lada!" and he ran out of his hideaway. Frightened Lada quickly put on her mice-coat and the wimple on her head and ran out. She recognized the prince' voice very well.

Hostivít met her in the door, embraced her and locked her mouth with a warm kiss so that she could not resist any longer.

"Now we will go to my father, darling," Hostivít said and wanted to lead Lada to the castle. But she did not want to saying: "I will not go to your father in this dress. Wait here for a short while until I come back again."

The prince wanted to object to many things but Lada was already behind the garden and she ran to the spring as a shy antelope. She found all her dresses, but the wail was missing and the little guard had also disappeared. But the happy bride did not have time to contemplate over this. She did not need the veil any longer and the loss was therefore not painful. She hurried with the bundle back to her cubicle, changed her clothes for a royal dress there, and after that she went to the dear prince who led her to his father. Those who met them wondered, told the others and the news about finding the beautiful lady spread around the whole castle.

Lada did not confide anything about her state to anybody until they came to the King. He blessed their marriage pleased even more knowing that his son had found a princess of royal origin.

The cook was going mad in the kitchen meanwhile. He grumbled that the kitchen miss had not come back. Then a servant came and called him to the prince. The cook threw off his apron quickly, cleared up his face and hurried upstairs. And he saw the King, the prince and the beautiful future Queen.

"Why do you keep such an ugly, dusted kitchen miss in the kitchen?" the prince thundered at him.

The cook was scared and started to beg: "Oh my merciful King and lord! I did not want to accept her but she begged so urgently that I could not send her away. And I do not have a more devoted, quick and diligent person than her in the whole kitchen. She only wears the mice-coat all the time, dusts herself all the time and is a little curious."

"Your blame is just, dear cook. And I thank you for the praise as well as for the sincere help. Your kitchen miss will reward you for that." So said Lada and the cook knelt at her feet, thanked her and asked for pardon because he recognized her voice. Lada calmed

him and gave him a poach of money in return. As soon as the cook left, everybody got to know who the mice-coat was, and were deadly afraid of her revenge when she became the Queen. But she did not think about revenge.

The engagement of the lovers took place soon after that. Then they all got on a carriage and went to the father of the beautiful bride to get a blessing from him. Lada entered the castle with awe and was afraid of her father's revenge. All in vain! The very night when she had disappeared from the castle, the late Queen revealed herself and had admonished his sinful love. Since that moment the King's heart had turned, the forbidden love disappeared and the former warmhearted father's love settled in him. He would have looked for his daughter long before but the late Queen forbade that and guarded her herself.

The King welcomed the daughter and the son-in-law with utmost joy and their happiness was his solace.